MW01132275

# Last One Standing

## The Chronicles of Kerrigan, Volume 11

### W.J. May

Published by Dark Shadow Publishing, 2016.

This is a work of fiction. Similarities to real people, places, or events are entirely coincidental.

LAST ONE STANDING

**First edition. May 15, 2016.**

Copyright © 2016 W.J. May.

Written by W.J. May.

# Also by W.J. May

**Bit-Lit Series**
Lost Vampire
Cost of Blood
Price of Death

**Blood Red Series**
Courage Runs Red
The Night Watch
Marked by Courage
Forever Night

**Daughters of Darkness: Victoria's Journey**
Huntress
Coveted (A Vampire & Paranormal Romance)
Victoria

**Hidden Secrets Saga**
Seventh Mark - Part 1
Seventh Mark - Part 2
Marked By Destiny
Compelled
Fate's Intervention
Chosen Three

**The Chronicles of Kerrigan**
Rae of Hope
Dark Nebula
House of Cards
Royal Tea
Under Fire

End in Sight
Hidden Darkness
Twisted Together
Mark of Fate
Strength & Power
Last One Standing
Rae of Light

**The Chronicles of Kerrigan Prequel**
Christmas Before the Magic

**The Hidden Secrets Saga**
Seventh Mark (part 1 & 2)

**The Senseless Series**
Radium Halos
Radium Halos - Part 2
Nonsense

**The X Files**
Code X
Replica X

**Standalone**
Shadow of Doubt (Part 1 & 2)
Five Shades of Fantasy
Glow - A Young Adult Fantasy Sampler
Shadow of Doubt - Part 2
Four and a Half Shades of Fantasy
Full Moon
Dream Fighter
What Creeps in the Night
Forest of the Forbidden
HuNted

Arcane Forest: A Fantasy Anthology
Ancient Blood of the Vampire and Werewolf

The Chronicles of Kerrigan

# Last One Standing

Book XI

By

W.J. May

Copyright 2016 by W.J. May

This e-book is licensed for your personal enjoyment only. This e-book may not be re-sold or given away to other people. If you would like to share this book with another person, please purchase an additional copy for each recipient. If you're reading this book and did not purchase it, or it was not purchased for your use only, then please return to Smashwords.com and purchase your own copy. Thank you for respecting the hard work of the author.

All rights reserved. No part of this publication may be reproduced, stored in or introduced into a retrieval system, or transmitted, in any form, or by any means (electronic, mechanical, photocopying, recording, or otherwise) without the prior written permission of both the copyright owner and the above publisher of this book.

This is a work of fiction. Names, characters, places, brands, media, and incidents are either the product of the author's imagination or are used fictitiously. Any resemblance to actual person, living or dead, events, or locales is entirely coincidental. The author acknowledges the trademarked status and trademark owners of various products referenced in this work of fiction, which have been used without permission. The publication/use of these trademarks is not authorized, associated with, or sponsored by the trademark owners.

## All rights reserved.
## Copyright 2016 by W.J. May
## Cover design by: Book Cover by Design

No part of this book may be used or reproduced in any manner whatsoever without written permission, except in the case of brief quotations embodied in articles and reviews.

# The Chronicles of Kerrigan

Book I - *Rae of Hope* is FREE!
  Book Trailer:
  http://www.youtube.com/watch?v=gILAwXxx8MU
  Book II - *Dark Nebula*
  Book Trailer:
  http://www.youtube.com/watch?v=Ca24STi_bFM
  Book III - *House of Cards*
  Book IV - *Royal Tea*
  Book V - *Under Fire*
  Book VI - *End in Sight*
  Book VII – *Hidden Darkness*
  Book VIII – *Twisted Together*
  Book IX – *Mark of Fate*
  Book X – *Strength & Power*
  Book XI – *Last One Standing*
  Book XII – *Rae of Light*
  PREQUEL – Christmas Before the Magic

# Chronicles of Kerrigan Prequel

A Novella of the Chronicles of Kerrigan.
A prequel on how Simon Kerrigan met Beth!!
NOW AVAILABLE:

# Find W.J. May

Website:
http://www.wanitamay.yolasite.com
Facebook:
https://www.facebook.com/pages/Author-WJ-May-FAN-
PAGE/141170442608149
Newsletter:
SIGN UP FOR W.J. May's Newsletter to find out about new
releases, updates, cover reveals and even freebies!
http://eepurl.com/97aYf

# Description:

*Last One Standing is the 11th Book of W.J. May's bestselling series, The Chronicles of Kerrigan.*

Rae Kerrigan and her friends have finally crossed the line, and this time, there's no going back. After a violent standoff with the entire Privy Council, the gang wakes up under the protection of the last people they ever expected to see: the Xavier Knights.

Old bridges are burned. New alliances are formed. There's a storm brewing on the horizon, and unless they unite together—it will overtake them all. What they need, is time. But an unexpected visit from an old enemy sets off a spark, and suddenly, Rae's entire world is in flames.

Can she and her friends get the people they need together in time? Even if they can, will they ever be strong enough? More importantly, are she and Devon strong enough to survive what's about to come?

A dangerous game has begun and the only question that remains is: who will be the last one standing?

# Chapter 1

*If you so choose, even the unexpected setbacks can bring new and positive possibilities. If you so choose, you can find value and fulfillment in every circumstance.*

*Ralph Marston*

*Yeah...I'd like to see that guy get stabbed in the stomach.*

Rae opened her eyes a little at a time, testing out them out slowly. She didn't understand much of what was going on around her.

To start, instead of being crumbled in an underground office somewhere, bleeding out on the floor, she was in a hospital bed of some sort. A rather nice hospital bed, where someone had supplied her with a generous stash of extra blankets and pillows. Warm sunlight streamed in from a row of windows lining the far wall, and from what she could see from beyond her curtain, there were other beds similar to hers, stretching all the way out to the door.

Yet, she wasn't in a hospital.

The beeping machinery above her and the wires strung across her body like Christmas lights were all hospital-grade, to be sure, but she'd been in enough infirmaries to know the difference. She was in a state-of-the-art facility somewhere. Except it wasn't anywhere official. And from what blurry fragments she remembered of her Privy Council-welcome yesterday, she was pretty sure it wasn't at Guilder. Which begged the question...

"Where the hell am I?" she muttered, her mouth dry and her lips cracked as she moved them.

Her tongue stuck in her throat, and she tried to rub it against the roof of her mouth, with no success. She had been palsied by drugs and shock, and while she couldn't yet put her finger on it she had a nagging suspicion that there was something strange going on in her lower abdomen.

Before she could twist around to find out, the biggest surprise of all floated into view, haloed by the lights above her head.

*Devon.*

Her mouth fell open in child-like confusion as her brow creased. "You're..."

"You're awake," he interrupted frantically. His voice had that manic tone she knew too well. The one where he was trying desperately to control his emotions and appear calm, but the edges of all his sentences were still tilted in panic.

*Oh, my poor Devon. You wear your heart on your sleeve. How is it that you ever became a spy?*

The corners of her lips tilted up and she tried again. "You're—"

"Hold on, Rae, don't try to talk. I'm going to get you some water, okay?" A warm hand slipped behind her head and helped prop her up towards a plastic cup. A gentle stream was coaxed into her mouth and she swallowed gratefully. "How's that? Do you want some more?"

"You're—"

"Let's try for some more, okay? Just a little bit. I know you don't want to, but the sooner we get you drinking liquids, the better you're going to—"

"*Devon.*" She cut him off with a smile and tried to catch her breath. "You're not hurt," she managed weakly, still studying his face.

"Nope," he glanced down at himself automatically before looking back up with an apologetic smile, "not this time."

"For once."

He gave a short, strained laugh. "Yeah, I thought of that."

She smiled again, before her eyes found his.

"And...you're here."

His face softened instantly and he knelt down so they were on the same level. "Of course I'm here. Where else would I be...but right here?"

He kissed her knuckles gently, and she realized they were holding hands.

"Julian texted you," she guessed, slowly piecing it all together. "In the park, that was you he was texting. He told me it was Carter..."

Devon smiled, stroking back her hair as delicately as though she was made of glass. "Of course he texted me. I've had him on paid retainer to spy for me ever since you graduated."

"I'll have to keep that in mind." Rae tried to laugh, but a sudden searing pain in her stomach made her reel back. "What...?" With trembling hands, she slowly peeled back her blanket to see a wide, blood-stained bandage peeking out the side of her hospital gown.

For a second, she just stared.

Strangely enough, it wasn't the severity of the wound or its debilitating location that had her so surprised. It was the fact that she had a wound to begin with.

In a drug-addled haze of complete confusion, she squinted painfully at the windows once more. It was morning. Morning light was streaming in from the east. She'd gone to Guilder the previous day. That meant that, in at least twelve hours, this cut still hadn't closed.

How...was that possible?

When she finally looked back up, Devon looked as pale as she felt.

"It was Mallins," he hissed in a shaky voice. "The bastard...he stabbed you." He seemed to be having a lot of trouble saying the word.

Rae was having just as much trouble turning it over in her foggy head. "*Stabbed* me...?"

It sounded ridiculous. Almost funny. Like some bad joke she or one of her friends would make about her insufferable ability to walk through a wood-chipper and live to tell the tale. It didn't sound like anything that could actually happen. Like anything that *had* happened...

Finally, she asked the only question her morphine-addled brain could compile. As simple as it was accurate.

"How?"

Devon's jaw clenched and his knuckles flashed white, but he kept his face a carefully controlled mask—free of all conflicting emotion. "He's a hybrid. I came in right as he said it. He's telekinetic, yes. That one we knew about. But his second power is an immunity of sorts. Your powers didn't work on him. My powers didn't work. So when *he* stabbed you..."

"...my healing power didn't work," Rae finished quietly. She considered this for a long time, eyes flickering occasionally to the window as she pieced things back together, one by one. "Well, at least now we know a way around my damn immortality, right? I know Mallins is already like a million years old, but we can keep him around just long enough for me to have a long and fulfilling life, and then when it's time, I can just ask him to smother me or something."

Devon was not amused. He simply squeezed her hand even tighter—the one he was still holding. The one she was willing to bet he hadn't let go of since they'd brought her here.

Whoever *they* were. And wherever *here* was.

She was about to ask, when she played back his words with a slight frown. "Wait...you said your powers didn't work on him either? What exactly did you—?"

"I don't need my powers to throw a good punch."

She looked up in shock. "You didn't..."

"I broke his nose. And his jaw. And possibly a whole mess of other things." For the first time since she'd opened her eyes, a look of vicious satisfaction cracked the carefully crafted bedside façade. "I would have finished him off completely if Fodder hadn't come inside at the same moment and pulled me off."

*Fodder.* She frowned again, trying and failing to pull herself higher up on the bed. What the hell was Luke doing there, and why was Devon calling him by his last name?

"Fodder...?" she asked softly, straining with the effort of trying to lift herself up. "What are you—?"

"Hey, let me help you with that," he said quickly.

A pair of soft hands reached down beneath the blankets and lifted her higher up on the pillows from her hips—putting no pressure at all on the wound. Once she was settled, he pulled his chair closer to the bed and gazed down at her with that same gentle smile. She forgot her question entirely and leaned back in contented exhaustion. She could stare at that smile for hours.

"I don't want you worrying about anything right now," he murmured, taking her hand once more and holding it in both of his own. "You just focus on getting better." He leaned in to brush back her hair again, and she saw the dark bruises of a sleepless night in the hollows beneath his lovely eyes. "I know you have questions, but just know that, right now, I promise you're in a safe place. I'm not going to let anything happen to you—"

"I know that," she interrupted quietly.

She didn't mean to speak in such a low voice; quite the contrary. But for the life of her, she couldn't seem to pull in enough air to make the words even a little louder. It simply took too much energy. Energy she didn't have.

But now was no time for weakness. Shell-shocked and sluggish as her mind was, she needed to know what happened yesterday. She needed to put it together.

She squeezed Devon's hand again. "Please tell me. I can handle it. Fodder—"

As if on cue, the door opened and Rae heard a pair of footsteps coming their way. Devon's ears perked up as well, but he didn't change his position. Instead, he simply angled himself slightly towards the curtain as his shoulder fell with an inaudible sigh.

"Looks like you're about to find out."

The curtain pulled back, and in walked a man who looked exactly like Luke...only thirty or so years older. Rae stared at him curiously for a moment, before her skin turned pale.

"Oh, no...how long was I out?"

Much to her surprise, the man chuckled softly. Even Devon had to smile.

"Rae Kerrigan, meet Mr. Anthony Fodder. He's Luke's dad." Devon seemed a bit reluctant to go on, and Mr. Fodder shot him a bemused glance. "And...the Commander of the Xavier Knights."

Rae blinked in amazement, not entirely certain whether the drugs were starting to get on top of her a bit. "Well, Luke certainly neglected to mention that."

Devon laughed softly. "Molly's all over it. Apparently, he also neglected to mention her to his family—for obvious reasons. So tensions around here have been pretty high..."

Standing behind them, Fodder cleared his throat and Rae hurried to extend her hand. It was difficult, what with the tangle of wires stuck to her body. Even more difficult with the loss of blood and the fact that her entire stomach had been essentially cut in half.

But the second she started trying, Fodder rushed forward to make up the difference. Her hair went flying back at the speed of the movement, and she understood—even before she felt—what his particular tatù was. It was the exact same ink as a boy named Riley who had graduated a year before her. Speed. More particularly, the speed of a cheetah.

"Miss Kerrigan," he shook her hand incredibly gently, eying her speculatively all the while, "I'm very glad to see you're doing better."

Over the years, Rae had made an unofficial science of determining how a person felt about her, and where they stood in the world of tatùs by how they said her last name. It had gotten to the point where she could pretty much figure if just the word 'Kerrigan' had blown any attempt at an understanding in the first few minutes. But Mr. Fodder was not so easy a read. He was thoughtful and serious, sure. But her name was neutral. Like he was waiting to be swayed either way.

She realized now that the chuckle she'd heard earlier was a rare thing. This was not a man who smiled often. Not that he was harsh, but he was most certainly stern. And not at all friendly.

Not at all like his son. Luke was a virtual ray of sunshine, smiling every day.

"Thank you," she murmured, trying to pull herself even higher and get a handle on what was going on. The opiates they had been pumping into her system weren't making it very easy. "I'm sorry. I'm not really sure what's—"

"They have you on a high dose of morphine," he interjected, eyeing her IV with a trace of sympathy. "I would imagine things are still a bit fuzzy. You had already lost a rather phenomenal amount of blood by the time we found you."

"You found me..." Rae repeated, eyebrows pulling together as she stared up at him. "Devon said you pulled him off of Mallins. You," she couldn't believe what she was about to say, "*you* were at Guilder?"

The Commander of the Xavier Knights rescued Rae Kerrigan from the President of the Privy Council on Guilder grounds. It had certainly been a day for the history books. Shame that Rae couldn't seem to remember any of it.

Fodder leaned back and stared at her inquisitively. "I got a rather interesting phone call from my son. Seems there have been lot of things he's failed to mention over the last few years. Like who exactly he's been spending his time with. Or why—as perhaps the first favor I believe he has ever asked of me—he requested that I gather up my best men and storm the halls of Guilder."

Rae shrank back into the pillows as she and Devon shared a quick look.

"You can imagine my surprise," Fodder continued in a brisk tone, "and the natural questions that emerged."

To be honest, Rae couldn't imagine. Not even a little bit. She was still stuck on the fact that Luke's own dad was the Commander of the Xavier Knights. And then the fact that he'd kept everything they'd been doing a secret all these years?

For Pete's sake! Luke had gone to San Francisco on a whim to save the day. He'd been struck into a coma and had freaking brain surgery! He and Molly had been together longer than any relationship either of them had ever had before.

And the gang teased *Luke* for not technically being a spy?!

*Pshh*! He was better than all of them combined.

"Yeah," she finally answered in a small voice, "I can imagine that would be...quite a shock."

Fodder studied her face before continuing. "Fortunately, for all the things he may have kept from me, my son's word is still above reproach. When Luke told me it was life or death, I took a contingent of guards and headed straight for Guilder. I arrived just as Mr. Wardell was...well, let's say I arrived just in time."

Devon's lips pulled up in a humorless smile. "Actually, I would have preferred you were a minute or so early."

Fodder ignored this and turned back to Rae. "I understand that you've been through an unspeakable trauma, Miss Kerrigan, and I don't want to push you any further. When you've gotten your strength up, you and I can talk about what comes next. In the meantime, I suggest you rest. You and your friends are in good hands."

With that, he flashed a polite smile and left the room. Devon's eyes followed after him, before returning with concern to Rae. But Rae was still stewing in his departing words.

*...you and I can talk about what comes next...*

What did come next? They were a bunch of disbanded PC agents who had somehow washed up in a stronghold of the Xavier Knights. Luke's father or not, she wasn't exactly sure their circumstances had improved much. At any rate, she had no idea what that particular discussion would entail.

Then, just as she was thinking it over, her brain suddenly awakened to a far greater problem. "Devon!" she gasped, horrified the drugs had stopped her from putting it together sooner, "what happened to everyone else? Where's Molly?! Where're Gabriel and Angel?! Where's Julian?!" She tried to throw her legs over the side of the bed, but pulled back with a stifled scream.

Not once in her entire life had she felt such pain. It was blinding. Mind-numbing. Literally debilitating. She hardly even noticed as Devon swept her off her feet and laid her gently on the mattress. She was shaking so hard, she hardly even noticed when he reached across her and pressed the button to increase her flow of drugs. It wasn't until the fresh wave of morphine was coursing through her system that her head cleared enough for her to remember to breathe.

"So..." she finally panted, gripping Devon's wrist like her life depended on it, "this is what recovery is like, huh? All this time, I thought you guys were just being wimps."

"Please don't joke when you're like this." His face tightened in pain every bit as real as hers as he held tight to her trembling hands. "I can't take it..."

Her head bowed to her chest as she pulled in a steadying breath. When she looked back up, there were pre-emptive tears in her eyes. "Devon, tell me they're all okay."

He bit his lip. The same thing she did when she was hiding something.

"Molly and Julian are already up," he said quickly. "Both had concussions, and Jules broke his arm and his nose, but whatever drugs they gave to sedate them wore off a couple hours ago."

Half of Rae's heart leapt for joy, the other half was still frozen in fear. "And...Gabriel? Angel?"

It came back to her in bits and pieces. Flashes from the fight. Angel had been knocked to the ground with a force great enough to dent a car. Rae still remembered the torrents of crimson blood running through her white hair. How could she have come back from that?

And Gabriel...?

Her throat tightened and a dozen tears slipped down her cheeks. The bullet Gabriel had taken had been meant for her. He had leapt in between her and a gunman as she'd run to the Oratory. She flinched as she remembered the moment of impact. Right in his chest. Right in his heart, for all she knew. The shot meant for her...

"Angel is..." Devon stopped short, and tried to collect himself. "She's stable, right now. I mean, that's what the doctors all say. They don't know if..."

Rae squeezed his hand and forced him to look at her. "Just tell me."

He bowed his head and nodded. "Rae, they don't know if either one of them is ever going to wake up. With Angel, they're calling it blunt-force trauma. Any more force and it would have killed her for sure. As it stands, either she wakes or she doesn't."

Rae's head nodded quickly. Or maybe she was just shaking that hard. "And Gabriel?"

"The bullet missed his heart by four centimeters. They went in and repaired everything they could, but..." He sighed. "...but he basically bled out at the scene. If he wakes, they're not sure what kind of shape he's going to be in. If there will be brain damage. Whether or not he'll know his own name. And that's *if* he wakes."

*Because he came with me. Because I called him.*

The bright, sunlit walls of the makeshift hospital felt like they were closing in. There was a pounding in Rae's head she was finding impossible to ignore. Something she doubted had anything at all to do with her incision.

"Hey," Devon said sharply, causing Rae to shoot her gaze up to him, "I know that look. And I'm not going to have it. Not even for an instant, do you hear me? Angel and Gabriel are adults. They went there of their own volition for something they believed in. This was the price they paid for the risk they took. It has nothing to do with you. Molly and Julian are the same way."

Another stream of tears poured down Rae's cheeks and she pulled in a painful breath. "You wouldn't say that if our positions were reversed. You would see where the blame should—"

"It cheapens it, d'you hear me?" Gone was the gentle, accommodating Devon who'd rushed to get her water and held her hand. The man before her was as unshakable and determined as they come. "It cheapens what they did and what they sacrificed if you try to put it on yourself. I'm not going to let you do that. It's not your blame. And it's not your right."

She felt like he'd slapped her in the face. But it wasn't cruel or harsh. It was like he'd slapped her awake. He was right, she realized. Just like usual, Devon was right.

She nodded hastily and he regarded her with a critical eye.

"Do you understand?" he demanded. "Say you understand."

"I understand."

He leaned back, looking satisfied. A second later, he slipped his hand into hers once more.

Her eyes lingered on their intertwined fingers for a long time as the new wave of drugs quickly took hold. Her eyelids were becoming impossible to keep open, and if it wasn't for a sudden explosion down the hall, she might have fallen fast asleep.

"What was that?" she gasped, clutching her stomach in pain as she tried to sit up.

Devon was on his feet at once, angling himself automatically between the door and her bed.

"I don't know," he answered, on high alert. "Maybe the PC is retaliating. Maybe the—"

"WHERE THE HELL IS SHE?!"

There was another crash, this one was louder than before.

"YOU WANT TO END UP A BRISKET LIKE YOUR FRIEND?! YOU TELL ME WHERE THE HELL MY DAUGHTER IS RIGHT NOW!"

Devon slowly relaxed his posture with the hint of a smile. "You know, your mom really knows how to make an entrance."

"Yep." Rae sank back into the pillows with an apologetic grimace. "This is going to go a long way towards solidifying our new tentative relationship with the Knights..."

There was a deafening bang outside the infirmary door, followed by a flash of blue light.

"OVERREACTING?! LET ME TELL YOU SOMETHING, HONEY, YOU HAVEN'T SEEN OVER-REACTING! NOW, IF YOU DON'T STEP AWAY FROM THAT DOOR, I'M GOING TO—"

"Mom?" Rae called tentatively.

The shouting stopped at once, and, rather anti-climactically, the door creaked open to reveal a tear-stained Beth. The second she saw her daughter, she was beside the hospital cot in a flash, weeping openly as she fussed and questioned and prodded, and generally did whatever it was mothers were supposed to do in this situation.

Rae soaked in all the attention a little smugly—sniffing all the while for fire-damage—until Carter filed quietly inside as well. Their eyes locked and Rae's jaw fell open in amazement.

It was one thing for her mother to be here. Her mother no longer worked for the Council and was, well, her *mother*. But Carter? The President of the Privy Council in the den of the Xavier Knights?! How the hell did that work?!

"What are you doing here?" she breathed over her mother's head. She was still too weak to pull in a full breath, and Beth's frantic hovering wasn't helping.

Devon turned around, and even Beth pulled back to stare at Carter.

He was standing with his hands stuck deep in his pockets, looking like he hardly knew the answer himself. Things were moving here at the speed of light, and in the end it was Beth who answered Rae's question.

"Julian called him, too. But just like Devon, he got there too late."

*Carter had been there?*

Rae shook her head weakly. "I'm sorry, I don't...I don't remember."

"That's okay, honey." Beth knelt by the side of the bed and took the hand that Devon wasn't currently holding. "All that matters is you're safe now." She closed her eyes and repeated it again, almost to herself. "You're safe."

But Rae couldn't understand it. By her side, Devon wasn't having any more luck.

"But...how is it that they're allowing you here?" he asked quietly, giving Carter a curious stare. "I don't even know why they're letting me, and you're the—"

"Well, I may not have arrived in time to help you and your friends," Carter cut him off suddenly, "but I did arrive in time to be permanently disavowed from the Privy Council."

Rae and Devon flashed twin looks of shock.

"What the hell for?!"

Carter flashed Rae a small smile.

"For trying to kill Victor Mallins."

# Chapter 2

Rae slept in the hospital wing that night. Or at least, she was supposed to sleep.

A little earlier that day, the doctor in charge had come by to take a look at her. The doctor was an incredibly efficient, though professionally cold, woman named Dr. Roscoe. The bandage on her stomach had been pulled back, and for the first time Rae was able to see the damage with her own two eyes.

It looked like a nightmare!

Devon and Carter were banished immediately behind the curtain, but Beth refused to budge and gazed down with an almost critical eye. Not usually one to be squeamish, even Rae found herself bracing against the mattress, watching with wide eyes as Dr. Roscoe prodded here and there, scribbling things down all the while. When she noticed the look of abject terror on the face of her patient, the doctor smiled. Not that it looked comforting in any way.

"This is all dried blood," she explained quietly, taking a cloth and gently wiping it away. "It makes it look worse than it is."

Rae watched in wonder as the grisly mess was quickly and expertly reduced to a single thin line, only a few inches long. Sealed with neat white stitches.

Whether it was the drugs or the fact that she'd never had a long-lasting injury before, she felt almost a little let down.

"That's *it?*" She stared down at it doubtfully. How could so small a thing cause so much damage? Cause so much pain? There had to be something here they were missing.

Beth's eyes softened in amusement, and even the unshakable doctor offered a faint smile.

"That's it." She tossed the bloody cloth onto a nearby counter and began unrolling a bundle of bandages. "Pretty incredible, huh?"

Rae frowned. "Maybe it went all the way through to the other side or something..." She resisted the urge to feel her back for a similar wound, but refused to believe that she had been taken down by something just a little longer than her pinky. "You know," she continued hopefully, "a through-and-through? Like a gunshot?"

Outside the curtain, she saw the silhouette of Carter smack Devon, who hastily turned his laugh into a cough.

Dr. Roscoe gave her a quick look before deliberately dressing and re-bandaging the wound. "Is this your first time in a hospital?"

Rae rolled her eyes at Beth and chuckled softly. "Hardly. Over the years, I've probably been in a room like this almost as many times as you. But this is my first time getting treatment."

Roscoe looked up with a frown. "What is that supposed to mean? The PC didn't treat you?"

"There was no need," Rae explained. "I have a healing tatù. Works on everything." Her eyes flickered down to where fresh blood was leaking through the gauze. "Well, almost everything."

"I see." Roscoe pursed her lips, and looked for a moment like she wanted to nick the corner of Rae's arm just to see it for herself. But instead, she merely placed her tools in the sink and pulled back the curtain to allow the men back inside. "Well, everything looks good. The blade sliced through the muscles in your stomach—that's why it's so painful—but it was a clean cut. For that, you should be grateful."

Beth raised her eyebrows at the choice of word and Devon growled, "Grateful?"

Roscoe ignored them. "I'm going to check on you one more time later tonight, and tomorrow morning we start your physical therapy. Alright?"

"Physical therapy..." Rae repeated. "Like...training and stuff?" She tried to flex her stomach and pulled back with a grimace. "I mean, I guess we could start with hand-held weapons and stuff, I'm just not sure if I'll be up for a full aerobic regimen by tomorrow—"

"*Walking,* Miss Kerrigan." Roscoe looked at her like she was nuts. "By physical therapy, I meant we're going to help you out of bed and get you *walking.*" She headed out of the infirmary, shaking her head all the while. As she vanished through the door, they heard her murmur, "What the hell do they do over there at the Privy Council...?"

Carter turned back to both Rae and Devon with a dry smile. "Do you feel like the Council pushed you kids too hard, too fast?"

Both of them adopted instant poker faces.

A thousand images flashed through Rae's head. Fifteen-year-olds hurling spears at one another. Jumping off the roofs of buildings. Infiltrating the royal family. Falling off cliffs and being chased by maniacal gunmen...

"No..." Rae shook her head with a frown.

Beside her, Devon scoffed. "Us? Please."

"Hey! You heard the doctor. Everybody out," Beth commanded. She kissed Rae on the forehead before gesturing the men to the door with a flaming hand. "Rae needs her rest."

Carter complied immediately, but Devon ducked beneath the smoke and doubled back to the bed for a quick kiss. Rae was stunned by the speed at which it happened. Even more shocked that it happened at all. She was still registering it when he pulled away with a nervous smile.

"I'll, uh..." His eyes searched hers. "I'll see you tomorrow, Rae."

She blinked up with a morphine-induced grin, feeling sixteen years old again. "Uh, sure...okay."

"*Now,* Wardell."

This time Devon hurried off behind Carter and Beth as they filed out, but tossed her a mischievous wink before the door closed.

Rae lay there in sudden silence. Her fingers drifted up to her mouth as she remembered the feeling of his lips on hers. So familiar. And yet so...

Weren't they broken up? Didn't they have good reasons for being broken up? And speaking of broken up, wouldn't it be...

*...maybe I should conjure some ice cream.*

Okay, that last one was the morphine talking.

In complete and utter exhaustion, Rae fell back against the pillows and closed her eyes, more than ready to let this unending day finally come to a close.

Except...the night had other plans.

Six hours later, she was still awake, her blue eyes burning metaphorical holes into the ceiling. Long gone was the novelty of being trapped in a hospital bed. Long gone was any trace of self-pity she had left. Dr. Roscoe had come and gone, the sun had already begun to set, and more than anything else in the entire world Rae wanted to see her friends.

She waited until the jingling keys of the pharmacist had faded at the other end of the hall before lifting herself slowly to a sitting position. It was just as bad as she remembered, from when she tried it the first time with Devon, and she jammed her fist in her mouth to keep herself from screaming.

*Should have done this when the morphine was still fresh in my system. Rookie mistake.*

But, in a way, Rae was grateful for the respite from the drugs, no matter how brief. She needed her mind clear. She needed to figure out what their next move was, what she was going to say in this fast-approaching meeting with Luke's father. Most importantly, she needed to go and see Angel and Gabriel for herself.

It was slow work—one hand over the other, pulling herself to the edge of the mattress at an infuriatingly glacial speed. Once she was there, standing up was another matter altogether. Twice, she had to resist the urge to conjure herself another syringe of painkillers right then and there. Twice, she almost texted Devon for help.

But she sensed that, of this particular nighttime endeavor, he would not approve. She was in no condition to fend off anyone who might try to stop her, and she needed to get this done.

One step. Then another. Then a shuffling of two more.

She was gripping the railing like her life depended on it, but it was working. She was making her way across the room. When she got to the counter, she found exactly what she was looking for: a small 'emergency exits' map that gave her the rundown of the facility. It was as she'd hoped. Her recovery room was just a few doors down from the ICU. With any luck, she could make it there and back without anyone being the wiser...

Just to be safe, she slipped into her prized invisibility tatù when she opened the door. Of course, that didn't quite explain the scattered drops of blood trailing out behind her, but hey, not her problem. The slight slope of the hallway made it even harder to walk than the flat surface in her room, but there was a wooden railing along the side, and before she knew it she was at the door to the ICU. Lifting up painfully on her toes, she peered inside.

There were no medical personnel in sight. In fact, it looked basically deserted. With a silent prayer for strength, she pushed the door open and slipped inside.

The blinds were closed tight so the English sunset couldn't get inside, and all the lights were off, giving the place an ominous sort of glow. The only sound Rae could hear was a pair of high-pitched alternating beeps coming from a set of monitors by the far wall. She drifted silently forward, drawn by the noise.

But the second she cleared the final curtain, she suddenly stopped.

She'd wanted to find her friends? Well, she'd just found them.

Angel and Gabriel were lying on twin beds. Brother and sister. Side by side.

Julian sat on a chair in between them. Much to Rae's surprise, he had one hand on each of them, like he was single-handedly holding the little family together. He didn't look up when she came in, and, judging by the blank, resigned look on his face, Rae guessed that he hadn't moved from that very spot since he woke up twelve hours ago.

"I feel like at any second, they'll just open their eyes," she whispered.

Julian jumped a mile and whirled around in his chair, scanning the darkened room behind him with slightly manic eyes. "Rae?"

*Oh, right. Invisible.*

She slipped back into sight and flashed him a look of apology. His heart rate slowed and he turned wearily back towards the beds.

"They won't," he said softly. "I've been thinking that for hours. But they won't."

"Jules, you don't know that." She shuffled up behind him and perched tentatively on his lap, gazing down at the two beds.

It was surreal. Like looking at them in a dream.

Both were perfectly postured, and perfectly still. Both practically shone with youthful beauty as they lay tethered to the beds by their IVs. Neither one had any visible injury. Neither one bore even a mark to suggest why they might be in such a state. It was as if they had merely fallen asleep.

Rae glanced behind her and squeezed Julian's leg. "You don't know that," she said again.

But that...seemed to be the problem.

"You're right," he said painfully. "I don't."

Unlike his two sleeping friends, every inch of Julian's body seemed to bear witness to the attack. There were deep bruises on both sides of his face, along with a sharp cut across his nose where Rae remembered Devon saying he broke it. His hands and neck were littered with a series of strange lacerations, and his right arm was layered in a stiff, black cast.

"I can't see if they're going to wake up," he continued. "Either one of them. I keep trying but...it's like it's out of their control."

Rae bit her lip and nodded, refusing to cry even though her eyes were brimming with tears. "Looks like we're both powerless on this one."

For the first time, Julian glanced down at her stomach, pushing her gently to her feet so he could get a better look. His dark eyes flashed occasionally white as he looked her over, keeping half of himself fixed on the future, and half of himself there with her.

"Oh, Rae..." He winced sympathetically as he settled on the present. "It won't heal?"

She shook her head. "Mallins is immune to me, so my ink won't work either." Her eyes drifted again to the sleeping siblings. "We're just going to have to wait and see..."

With a silent nod, he pulled up another chair and they both settled in to do exactly that.

While Julian's eyes were drawn almost exclusively to Angel, Rae stared unabashedly at Gabriel. She didn't think she had ever seen him so still. Even the times when he'd been sleeping, he always seemed to have something up his sleeve. Like at any moment, he might spring awake and catch you looking, with that infamous twinkle in his eye.

But not tonight.

Tonight he was someplace that she couldn't reach him. Not her, or the doctors, or even his own unwavering determination could wake him from this sleep. It had him tight in its clutches, paling his skin and deadening every bone in his body.

The silence was deafening.

The stillness set her teeth on edge. And Rae didn't think she had ever been so terrified. A part of her was aching to reach out and touch him. Another part didn't think she could survive it if she did.

"Thank you," she finally spoke, breaking the quiet after what could have been minutes or even hours, "for texting Devon."

"Anytime." Julian gave her a sad smile before his eyes turned back to Angel. "At least one of us should get our happy ending. Right?"

The sudden pain that ripped through her was worse than Mallins knife.


Rae felt like she had only just climbed back into bed and closed her eyes, when the curtains ripped open and she was awakened by the bright morning sun. She squinted weakly and held up a protective hand, prepared to deliver a full night of dreams alibi to Dr. Roscoe. But instead of the doctor, it was Molly who was perched on the edge of her bed.

"Hey," Rae said in surprise, her voice scratchy from lack of use. "Good morning."

"Good morning." Molly gave her a tight smile. "How are you feeling?"

It was an interesting question. While the pain had abated slightly from the previous day, all of Rae's muscles had stiffened to the point where she doubted they would work at all. Perhaps she had overdone it with her late-night excursion.

*Great. And on the day I'm supposed to impress everyone by walking...* "I'm actually feeling quite a lot," she joked, wincing as she pulled herself straighter. "How about you? Devon said you got up yesterday?"

Now that she mentioned it, Molly didn't look so good. Yes, she was up and about, but there was something decidedly off about her. It could have been the ashen tint to her skin, or the hollowed out circles beneath her eyes. It could have even been the enormous burn stretching from her elbow to her neck. But Rae didn't think it was any of these things. Molly had been hurt before. This was just...different.

"I did," she answered shortly, "a little before Julian."

Even her voice was off.

Clipped. Splintered. Carefully contained.

"I'm sorry I wasn't here when you woke up," she continued, her eyes flickering down to the tight bandage wrapped around Rae's waist. "I wanted to be, I just...there's been a lot going on."

*Of course!*

"Oh yeah," Rae was suddenly animated, "Luke!"

Molly's head snapped up as all the color drained from her face. "What about him?" she asked sharply.

Rae hesitated, a little thrown by her lack of enthusiasm. Usually, Molly was so full of excessive emotion it tended to spill out onto everyone around her.

"His dad..." she continued tentatively, eying her friend with more and more concern. "I can't believe his dad is the Commander of the Knights."

"Oh, yeah. That." Molly looked a bit relieved. "Yeah, I couldn't believe it either. Some coincidence, huh?"

"Worked out pretty well for us, though. If he hadn't called them..."

She trailed off and both girls fell quiet.

They stared at the clock. They stared at the machines. They stared anywhere but at each other. Rae didn't understand exactly why. She wasn't even sure if Molly really noticed.

Finally, when it could go on no longer, she tried again. "They're going to start my physical therapy today."

For the first time, Molly showed a bit of emotion. "Physical therapy? Already?" she asked disapprovingly. "You mean like training and stuff? Rae, if this doctor is being too hard on you, just say the word and I'll—"

"No," Rae chuckled gingerly. "In the land of the Knights, physical therapy apparently means walking around..."

Molly raised an eyebrow, but let it go. "Well, that sounds thrilling. Good luck with that."

"Thanks." Rae grinned. "You know, there's a meeting later with Luke's dad and a couple other high-ranking Knights. I think they wanted to talk to us about—"

"Yeah, you know what? I think I'm just going to take it easy today." Molly got suddenly to her feet and started backing away. "Try to sleep for a few more hours."

Rae stared after her in surprise. "Are you sure?" Her face clouded. "Molls, did I...are you mad at me for what happened? I would totally understand if you were—"

"No! Not at all!" Molly shook her head quickly, eyes brimming with sincerity. "I swear. I'm just...not up for a big meeting. Not after everything that's happened."

Rae leaned back in relief. "Yeah—of course. Just take it easy. Try to get some sleep." The door opened and the sound of a dozen or so voices floated into the room as Molly melted quickly away to the far exit. "Molls, I'll see you later tonight?"

Molly's eyes flickered nervously to the crowd, but she nodded, flashing Rae a quick smile as she yanked open the door. "Yeah. See you tonight."

The second she vanished into the hallway, Mr. Fodder gave a cursory knock and then pulled back the curtain, flanked by six or seven other people.

"Miss Kerrigan," he greeted her politely, "how are you feeling this morning?"

Rae scooted up higher on the mattress and tucked the blanket around her waist, refusing to cringe at the pain in her abdomen.

"Much better, thanks." She was relieved to see Beth and Devon making their way towards her through the crowd. Carter was right on their heels. "You...wanted to talk? With everyone?"

Anthony Fodder's eyes were the exact same color blue as Luke's. A rare sky blue that you didn't see very often. But, unlike Luke's, even when he smiled at her, they were stern. "Only if you're feeling up to it. Your doctor assures me that the worst is behind you, but I know your mother was...of a different opinion."

Rae stifled a grin. Knowing her mother, that was probably understating it.

"I'll be just fine," she replied, more to Beth than to Fodder. "We can talk about whatever you like. You did my friends and me a great service, and I'm sure you have some questions..."

Fodder's eyes flashed with the hint of a smile, and Rae blushed. Now *she* was probably understating it.

"Very good." He pulled up a chair and took a seat, seemingly oblivious to the entourage of people behind him. This was a man who was firmly in control of whatever room he set foot in. He was there to obtain his objective, nothing more. It made Rae sit up a bit straighter. "To start, and in the interest of full transparency, I'd like to let you know that I already know everything about you, your school, your family, and your friends. This isn't from talking with my son; this is because my organization carefully monitors every active tatù—and being rather renowned agents of the Privy Council, the four of you were already quite high on our radar."

To be honest, Rae wasn't surprised in the slightest, only perhaps by the word renowned.

She knew the Knights had files on them, just like the PC had files on the Knights. She did appreciate him saying it, though. "Right, well," she cleared her throat, "also in the interest of full transparency, you should know that I don't speak for anyone or any organization here. I mean, I'm incredibly grateful for everything you've done, and I'll be happy to answer whatever questions you have, but—"

"Miss Kerrigan," he interrupted her softly, "neither I nor anyone else within my organization suffers any delusions about exactly who you are and what you represent. I wanted to talk with you for this very reason. So the two of us can build some sort of understanding."

*'Who you are and what the heck do you represent'?! Shit! And what was that exactly...?*

"Um..." she faltered, glancing automatically at Carter. "I'd like that, too?"

For the first time, Fodder offered her a faint smile. "To be honest, most people who know everything about my family want to have very little to do with me so..." She trailed off, wondering why she felt the need to volunteer that. She'd said it almost as a disclaimer. Maybe it was the drugs?

Fodder, however, leaned back in his chair and nodded as if this was perfectly normal. "I've never been one to judge the children for the sins of the father. Furthermore, I happened to know your father a little. He approached the Knights before he went out on his own. He was hoping to forge some sort of alliance."

Beth and Carter exchanged a covert look, but Rae's jaw fell open in honest amazement. *What?* "He did?"

"We approved of his research, just not his methods," Fodder explained. "The day we refused his offer of partnership was the last we ever heard of him."

Rae stared down at the mattress, trying to think of something to say, but Fodder leaned forward again and folded his hands upon his knees.

"But I don't want to talk about your father."

She looked up nervously, fingers fiddling with her newly inserted IV. "Okay...what do you want to talk about?"

"Let's start with something simple." He studied her critically, and the rest of the people behind him seemed to lean forward an inch or two. "What's on the computer?"

Rae blanked. Completely blanked.

"The computer?"

Fodder's eyes narrowed. "You deny there was a computer?"

"Whoa, whoa—she's not denying anything," Devon interjected, slipping past the threatening-looking men in front of him to come and stand at Rae's side. "Just give her a second to think. She did just get *stabbed,* you know," he added, shooting Fodder a pointed glare.

*The computer, the computer? Is he talking about my computer? But it's back at the penthouse. What computer is he—*

"Oh—the *laptop!*" Rae exclaimed suddenly. "Of course. It was Mallins' private laptop. I found it in his desk. It's the whole reason we went to Guilder. There was evidence on the drive that he and an older version of the Council conducted the exact same hybrid experiments as my dad. We needed it to expose him to the rest of the Privy Council."

Fodder's brow creased with a slight frown. "Why?"

By this time, both Luke and Molly had filed into the room and were standing quietly against the wall—both in separate corners.

*Why? Why indeed!*

Rae stared back at Fodder, wondering what sort of game he was playing at. "Because now is not the time for us to be divided. There's a storm coming, and we're all going to have to stand together if want to have any chance of winning this fight."

The room went quiet. Dead quiet. A quiet that seemed to crackle with pent-up hostilities as the ex-members of the PC and the Xavier Knights stared each other down.

Finally, Fodder spoke. "What fight?"

You could have heard a pin drop.

Then, strangely enough, every single person in the room turned at the same time...to Luke.

If he had an invisibility tatù, he would have used it then. His tan skin lightened to a guilty shade of chalk as he visibly resisted the urge to take a step back. Instead he stood tall, gazing back evenly at his father.

Rae couldn't believe it. Simply couldn't believe it.

Luke hadn't told the Knights about Cromfield. A player as big as that—a shift in the tatù world as big as that—he had kept to himself. To protect his friends. And Molly.

From the looks of things, Molly was just beginning to piece this together herself. Whatever strange dissonance was going on with her, it melted clean away as she stared at him with enormous, shocked eyes. Tiny tears sprang up, and the next second she was in his arms.

"I didn't think it mattered," he murmured, half to her, half to the room. "By the time I found out about him, he was already going underground. I thought...I thought we had time."

Mr. Fodder's face hardened infinitesimally, but he turned deliberately away, focusing instead on Rae. He would deal with his son later. "What fight?" he asked again quietly.

Rae took a deep breath, and decided to lay all their cards out on the table. After all, this fight didn't end with her and her friends. Or even the Privy Council for that matter. It belonged to anyone and everyone who was inked. Any child born into the world of tatùs. "Jonathon Cromfield. The fight is with Jonathon Cromfield. It's going to be bigger than a fight. A war."

Fodder drew in a sharp breath, and without seeming to mean it, his eyes flickered to her morphine drip. "The same Jonathon Cromfield who died over five hundred years ago?"

This time, Carter stepped forward. He understood Fodder's confusion, and the simple act alone lent an undeniable air of credibility to what Rae was saying. "He didn't die. He was a hybrid, gifted with immortality as well as sight."

It was quiet for a long time. A part of Rae was terrified that Fodder and the Knights simply wouldn't believe them—turn them back in for the PC to deal with however they saw fit. Another part was terrified they would believe them—terrified of what would happen next.

Fodder made no commitment either way. "We need to consider this," he said simply. "We'll discuss it as a group. In the meantime, it would help if you could give us any and all information you have on Cromfield. Any evidence that could prove he is still alive."

Rae bowed her head. "Well, that's going to be a problem."

"Why is that?"

She glanced up. "Because both of our resident experts are asleep in your medical wing with little chance of waking up."

But even as she spoke, there was a sound of pounding footfalls from down the hall. The door crashed open and Julian stood frozen in the frame, beaming with uncontrollable joy.

"Actually, I wouldn't be so sure about that."

# Chapter 3

According to the doctors, there was no earthly explanation for why Angel woke up. The head wound she sustained should have put her into a coma from which there would be no escape.

And according to the medical staff the Xavier Knights employed, even if she did somehow awake, the damage caused to her brain would be irreparable and have devastating effect—destroying the girl they once knew.

Clearly these doctors had never met Angel.

"I don't care what your instructions were—*I'm* the patient, so *I'm* changing them. Now you're going to take these wires off of me, or I promise you, sweetheart, you're going to end up exactly like your friend!"

Rae and the others ripped back the curtain and saw Angel half-risen from bed, tugging impatiently at two of the IVs still stuck inside her arm. One orderly stood frozen on the other side of the bed—looking rather terrified—and the other was cowering in the far corner, staying carefully out of reach of her threats.

The second she saw them, Angel stopped struggling. Her face relaxed into a huge smile which she gifted to each of them before settling on Julian. "*Finally*, honey. When you said you'd be right back, I had assumed that implied it would be in some sort of timely manner."

Julian laughed aloud and paced forward. With a look of profound tenderness, he knelt on the ground beside her bed and leaned in for a long kiss.

There was some awkward throat-clearing and eye-averting from Fodder and the Knights, but to Rae, the scene could not have been more natural. She thought her heart was going to burst with happiness for Julian. There was some good out of this nightmare. Cromfield, Mallins, and any other piece of crap that wanted to take them down wasn't going to succeed.

They had been through enough. Julian and Angel deserved whatever happiness they could find. And no one, *no one* was going to fault them for stealing precious little moments whenever or wherever they could get them.

As the two lovers finally parted, Devon lowered Rae gently to her feet. There was no way she would have been able to keep up with the crowd surging towards the hospital wing, so he had picked her up and carried her. She kept a steadying hand on him, as her eyes darted wildly around.

The curtains in the ICU had been pulled up around each of the beds, so she had no idea what was happening on the other side of the partition.

"And...Gabriel?" she asked hopefully, glancing first at the doctors and then at Julian for a response. There was nothing but silence and her cheeks flamed red as she lowered her eyes to the floor. As soon as she said it, she realized how stupid it was. She didn't know why she thought that one would affect the other. Of course they wouldn't.

It's just...it seemed like Angel and Gabriel did everything together.

They were taken together. They were raised together. They survived together.

Couldn't it stand to reason that they would wake up together too? Couldn't that, *please*, just once, be the way the world worked? Instead of all this?

"Sorry," she muttered, keeping her eyes on the ground. "...that was stupid."

Devon squeezed her hand, and when she looked up, even Fodder's face softened sympathetically. Angel, however, straightened up on high alert.

"What happened to Gabriel?" she asked sharply, daring each of the people in the room to meet her eyes. When no one did, she turned to Julian. Long gone was the gentle smile and her sarcastic sparkle. She looked like an avenging angel—out for blood. "*Jules.*" There was ice in her voice, and for the first time in a long while, Rae was reminded of the girl she'd met in the hotel room in San Francisco. The cold-blooded killer. "Where. Is. He?"

Julian's eyes flickered automatically to the other side of the curtain and he sighed. "He got shot, love. In the chest. The surgery was technically a success, but he hasn't woken up yet."

Just hearing the words said aloud made them all the more terrible. Rae's eyes welled with automatic tears, and for a moment, every other problem in the world seemed to fade away.

She didn't care about Cromfield, or the Privy Council, or whose side the Xavier Knights were going to decide to take. All she cared about was whether or not Gabriel Alden was going to open his eyes. It was the only thing that mattered.

"But he's going to, right?"

Angel's voice shattered her reverie and brought her back to the present. Despite having just woken up from a coma, the girl looked like she was about to set the whole building on fire with every Xavier Knight inside.

Dr. Roscoe, who had joined them in the infirmary when she heard all the commotion, put on her best 'temper-your-expectations' tone. "We're not sure yet. His body went through an unspeakable amount of trauma."

Angel didn't even blink. "And?" When Roscoe paused, she turned to Rae in frustration. "Do they not know *who* we are?"

Rae opened her mouth to answer, but the doctor cut her off. "I would simply recommend that you don't get your hopes too high. As resilient as you lot have proven, there's still an extremely limited possibility that he may ever wake up."

Julian and Devon flinched at the same time, but Angel's eyes flashed fire. "But that's what you said about me too, right?" The room went dead quiet as her words echoed away. "*Right*?!"

"That's right." Dr. Roscoe looked extremely uncomfortable.

"That's settled then." Angel leaned back against the pillows looking drained, but satisfied all at the same time. "He'll wake up. I know he will. Just give him a little time." She swallowed and blinked hard. "He was always a step or two behind me."

Rae wasn't sure if she imagined it or not, but she could have sworn that as she said it, Angel gave her a little reassuring wink.

"In the meantime," she completely bypassed the terrified-looking physicians and looked imploringly up at Julian, "I could really use some chocolate. Or maybe some wine?"

His dark eyes flickered to the look of fury twisting Roscoe's face. "Uh..."

Rae felt a soft poke in the ribs, and Devon lowered his lips to her ear. "I think that's probably our cue to get out of here."

With hushed and hasty murmurs of goodbye, he picked her up again and they were quickly followed the rest of the group outside into the hallway. The door was just swinging shut as they heard the beginnings of what promised to be an explosive argument regarding the Patient's Bill of Rights.

Now that Devon and Rae were alone again with Fodder and his group of not-so-merry men, Rae felt suddenly afraid. She didn't know exactly what she should be doing in this situation. She didn't know why it was that her opinion seemed to matter more than, say, Carter's. And perhaps most importantly, she noticed—from her perch in Devon's arms—that all the ex-members of the PC and the Xavier Knights were standing in two distinct groups. It was as if there was an invisible line that they were both only subconsciously aware of, but were both either unwilling or unable to cross. And yet, Devon and Rae stood in the middle.

Fortunately, Fodder stepped graciously forward to break the ice. "Well on behalf of both myself and Knights, I'm very pleased your friend is on her way to a recovery." An echo of Angel's profanities filtered through the door and the PC group collectively flinched. "A full recovery, from the sounds of it." Rae could have been mistaken, but she could have sworn she saw his lips twitch into a smile. "At any rate, we'll be holding several meetings to discuss the information you shared. In the meantime, I invite you all to take full advantage of our facilities here. Anything you need will be completely at your disposal. You need only ask."

With that, he turned sharply on his heel and marched away, followed by a company of his increasingly-menacing looking men.

Rae looked after them with a grin, but turned to surprise when she turned back to see the hard expression settling over Devon's face. "What's the matter?" she asked curiously. "You don't like it here?"

He shifted restlessly, arms tightening automatically around her. "No, it's not that. This is a state-of-the-art facility. We couldn't expect anything more."

"Then?"

His eyes fixed on the door that Fodder and his men had just disappeared through.

"Try asking them if we can leave."


Rae couldn't sleep again that night. Although exhausted to the point of delirium, she found herself tossing and turning just like the night before. It wasn't that anything in particular troubled her, by all measurable accounts, it had been a good day.

Angel had woken up, they'd finally laid all the cards out on the table for the Knights, and just that afternoon, Roscoe had given Rae permission to go outside the following morning.

Yet try as she might to count her blessings...none of that meant shit while Gabriel was still lying in the hospital.

Quiet as a mouse, she once again pulled herself to her feet and began the same nightly trek she had made the previous evening. This time, instead of finding the hallway deserted, groups of men and women walked past in tightly uniformed groups, one after another.

*There has to be some sort of training exercise going on,* she thought to herself, as she turned invisible and shrank back against the wall. Most of the people looked as young as she and her friends.

After a few minutes, the last group filed past. She was just about to creep forward once more, when some talking from the back of the ranks caught her attention and she hesitated slightly.

"...just went in there and busted them loose. Like they were one of us or something."

"I think it's good," a higher voice countered. "They probably would've died if the Commander hadn't done anything—"

"So go ahead and let them," the first voice interrupted. "What business is it of ours what goes on at that damn school? Why should we care?"

Rae froze in her tracks and turned around, trying to locate the source of the conversation.

"I just don't get it," another voice interjected. This one was clearly trying to be the rational mediator of the group, but he was spewing pure venom. "I know Luke is his son and everything, but I mean, look at who we're talking about. Molly Skye? The girl who could black out a city block if she put her mind to it? Julian Decker—the infamous psychic? *Devon Wardell*?! He's the most promising agent the PC has ever seen. Do you remember how long you were trying to break his marksmanship record? And *these* are the people we risked our lives to save?"

Rae saw them now. Two guys and a girl. All in their late teens. Engaged in a rapid, yet hushed discussion at the back of the line. The man who was talking shook his head disapprovingly.

"Gabriel Alden—we couldn't even get a file on that guy! The only thing we found was an unconfirmed report of a man fitting his description involved in a single-handed agency take-down in Southern Turkey. *Single-handedly* took out an entire agency. And the girl—Angel? She's a freaking ghost, man! No reports, no records, nothing but black holes and casualties. And of course...then we have bloody Kerrigan herself."

At this point, Rae leaned forward, actually rather interested to hear.

"The girl's a freak—a menace. No one person should have that much power, it's not natural. And the longer she stays in here, the greater the chance is that she'll take all our ink as well."

The girl, a short, curly-haired brunette, rolled her eyes. "First of all, let me say that it's a little counter-intuitive to talk about 'natural' when discussing superpowers." Rae stifled a grin; she liked this girl very much. "And second, not only has she done absolutely nothing to threaten us, but the poor thing can barely walk. She got stabbed through the stomach. She's not exactly in fighting form here—"

"But that's exactly my point," the guy who had been so threatened by Devon continued. He ran a hand through his greasy blond hair. "Do you want to wait for her to get back into fighting form? Do you really want her to be here when that happens?"

A collective shiver ran between them and even the girl fell thoughtfully silent. The first man who spoke was eager to join in on the hunt.

"Plus they're all sleeping with each other. It's just freaking weird."

*What?! Was this published somewhere?!*

But this time, the girl scoffed. "You're just jealous. I saw the look on your face when they carried in those girls. The two of you practically wet yourselves. Not that they'd be interested in any of you, of course..."

The men flashed each other a quick look, before the first one asked, "And why is that?"

"Oh please." She smirked and rejoined her place in line. "Did you see those *guys?*"

With that, the three of them walked away with their platoon, leaving Rae frozen in their wake. Wondering what exactly was in their files.

*Another day, Rae. One step at a time.*

Shaking it off as best she could, she made her way down to the ICU and peeked inside the door. All the curtains were pulled back now, and the room appeared deserted. In a similar streak of good luck, Angel had apparently worn herself out with all the cursing and screaming and was out cold with a rather self-satisfied look on her face.

Not that Rae didn't want to talk to her. She just...had other people on her mind.

She slipped inside without a sound and sat down on the chair next to Gabriel. He hadn't moved an inch since the last time she saw him. Each golden lock was splayed in exactly the same place across his forehead; each monitor chimed with the same, repetitious beeps.

Rae hated it. A part of her wanted to throw caution to the wind, unplug him from the wall, and carry him off far away from this place. He didn't belong in a place so sterile and cold. It wasn't right for him to be so still. He wasn't supposed to be strapped down to a bed...at least, not like this.

Despite the cold shadows that dripped off the mechanic furniture, Rae couldn't help but smile. If he had been awake, Gabriel would surely have made a joke about that.

Without stopping to think about it, she leaned forward and took his hand. Things had always been like that between them, she realized. They did things impulsively, acting and speaking without thought. And while it had admittedly gotten them into serious trouble on a few occasions, she honestly wouldn't trade it for anything in the world. It engendered a rare kind of honesty, one she wasn't sure she shared with anyone else on the planet. Not even Molly or Jules. Not even Devon.

"I wish you were awake," she whispered, lacing her fingers through his. His hand was ice cold and she rubbed it gently, her eyes drifting to the paned windows as she stared out into the dark night. "You'd know exactly what to say right now. You'd know exactly what to do. All these people, they're turning to me like I have answers but...well, I think you and I both know that's not true."

Her eyes flickered sideways and landed on his sleeping face.

"That was your cue. I was wide open there."

Nothing.

"No jokes? No mockery? I'll give you a free shot."

Silence.

A shudder ran through her body and she brought his knuckles up to her lips.

"Why did you do that?" she whispered. Her voice grew almost angry as her eyes welled up with tears. "Why did you jump in front of the bullet? You know it couldn't have killed me, but you?" She glanced at the wires and tubes stringing out from his body, and a sudden wave of uncontrollable anger rose her blood to a boil. "You had *no right* to save me like that. You had *no right* to be so reckless with yourself. I need you here—do you understand me? I need you alive. And awake."

A dry sob rattled through her chest as the tears began to fall. "*Please.*" Her head bowed to the floor, spilling her hair forward as she wiped at her cheeks with her free hand. "I need you, Gabriel. I need you to wake up."

But there was nothing but silence, and Rae sat slowly back in her chair.

She held on to Gabriel's hand for what felt like forever, crying silently as the peaceful night carried slowly on. She had no concept of time anymore. No concept of space. Her thoughts were focused on one thing, and one thing only.

*Please Gabriel...I need you to wake up.*

The monitors continued to beep and the soft noise of Angel's breathing continued. If Rae had the energy to sob she'd have tried.

She gasped and nearly dropped Gabriel's hand when a soft voice broke the never-ending stillness—a voice that brought her back to life.

"Well darlin', I thought you'd never ask."

# Chapter 4

In hindsight, it probably wasn't the best idea to jump on top of a man who'd recently been shot and underwent heart surgery, but Rae couldn't help herself. She didn't even consider the cut deep into her abs.

Truth be told, the thought of it being dangerous never even crossed her mind.

*"GABRIEL!"*

The word slurred slightly as her voice muffled in the blanket covering his chest. His body jerked back in pain, but he didn't pull away. Quite the contrary, aside from shifting her slightly so that her weight wasn't near his heart, he refused to let her go.

"That's what I call a warm welcome," he joked softy, winding his arms beneath hers. Rae couldn't tell whether the volume was intentional or not, but either way, he was talking.

"I can't believe it," she whispered, breathing in his warm citrus smell, "you're awake."

Beneath her, she felt him chuckle silently. "Well...you did call."

*Call? What the—?* "Wait," her brow creased into a frown, "how did you...? How is that even possible? I thought—"

"I heard your voice inside my head." He yawned and grimaced slightly. "You needed me to wake up."

When she pulled back, he was staring off into the distance with a very peculiar expression on his face. His hands tightened around her and he drew in a painful breath.

"At first, I thought I was dreaming. I think I was dreaming for a long time. And then...I heard you calling. You sounded so upset..." He trailed off again as he tried to piece it together. His sparkling eyes clouded for a moment as they followed the tubes trailing out from his wrists to where they plugged into the wall. A tentative hand came up to his chest, and for the first time, he seemed to register where he was. "Rae..." the voice was sharper now, though still weak, "did I get shot?"

"Oh Gabriel!" She wrapped her arms around him again as her eyes spilled over with tears. A second later, she felt his hand patting the back of her head.

"...I'm taking that as a *yes.*"

A watery laugh choked out of her, and she sat up on the side of the mattress, gazing down at him with red-rimmed eyes. "Yes, you got shot. In the chest. They had to do surgery."

He absorbed this with the impossible resilience of a child raised in a cave by a mad-man, eying the beeping monitors with an almost detached curiosity. "Really."

"It missed your heart by four centimeters," she whispered.

He flashed her a quick smile. "Well, in the shooter's defense, it's a very small target."

"Don't joke," her face fell into her hands, "it isn't funny."

"Oh come on," he peeked under his shirt to survey the damage, "it's a little bit funny."

"No it's not." She pulled in a shaky breath, staring down at him with a quiet sort of desperation—terrified that at any moment, his eyes might close again. "Do you...do you remember anything that happened?"

Instead of answering, he leaned his head back against the pillows with an exhausted sigh. She was highly unaccustomed to such displays of vulnerability, and it tore at her heart.

"Not really. Why don't you just tell me?"

*Tell you how you jumped in front of a bullet for me? Tell you how the computer got smashed in the skirmish and I ended up getting stabbed by some freakish power that I can't heal myself? Tell you that there's a likely chance we're being hospitably held as prisoners?*

"Um..."

He cracked a smile. "Just say it, Rae. It can't be that bad."

She rolled her eyes. "Really? After all these years, you really want to tempt fate like that?"

"Fair point. You're marked by fate wherever you go, best not tempt it sometimes." He watched and blinked slowly. "So how bad is it?"

But much as he deserved an answer, she couldn't bring herself to give it. Everything he had done had ended up being in vain. Everything he had sacrificed—irrelevant.

*But that's not the worst part, is it?*

A little voice chided in the back of her head, and she dropped his gaze. No, it wasn't the worst part. Not by a long shot. The worst part was this: Gabriel had jumped in front of a bullet to save her life...only to wake up and discover that she and Devon were back together.

Her cheeks flamed red and she tucked her hair nervously behind her ears. "Well, to start, you should know that everyone we went in with is okay—"

"So...it's him, huh?"

Her eyes snapped up in surprise. "What?"

"You and Devon. Back together."

It wasn't said as a question. And it wasn't said with the slightest bit of blame. In fact, he had asked her in the same tone he would use if debating where to get take-out or what movie they wanted to see.

Her lips parted uncertainly, and she suddenly wondered how much mental and emotional strain his heart could technically handle right now.

"How...did you know that?"

He gave her a measured stare for a moment, before his face softened into a grin. "You have that annoying, dreamy look about you."

"Annoying, dreamy—"

"Or maybe it's just all the blood loss."

A burst of laughter escaped her lips. "Yeah, that must be it. But yeah," her expression grew suddenly serious as she tried to measure his, "I believe we're back together."

A rather wistful look passed over his handsome face, before he nodded with a little shrug. "That...fits."

*That fits?* Rae shot him an incredulous look. "Are you serious?" Maybe this was the meds talking.

"Hey," he grinned, "every relationship needs at least one good affair. And I fully intend to be that person for you. In a way, it actually kind of frees me up—for the plotting."

She burst out laughing, clutching her sides in pain as she rocked back and forth. "You are the most—*ow*—the most incorrigible—*ow*—the most—"

"Hey!" He glanced over in alarm and looked down at the tight bandage wrapped around her stomach for the first time. "What the hell is that? Stop laughing," he commanded, gesturing her closer. As she leaned in, he yanked up the bottom of her shirt without a second thought. A tiny red stain had leaked through the bandages, and his face darkened in rage. "Who did that to you?"

As utterly bizarre as it sounded, for a split second, Rae almost felt a wave of sympathy for Mallins. She would have felt it for anyone who found themselves on the other end of that look.

"It turns out, Mallins is a hybrid," she explained softly. Gabriel refused to take his eyes off the wound. "His ability—other than telekinesis—is an immunity to tatùs. It meant that when he stabbed me—"

"He stabbed you."

Again, it wasn't a question.

Despite the fact that he had recently been shot himself, Gabriel forced his body into an upright position and began glancing about for his clothes.

"Where is he? Is he still back at Guilder?"

Rae stared at him in amazement. "Hang on a second—are you crazy? Gabriel, you just had open heart surgery! You shouldn't even be sitting, let alone—"

"Find me some pants." He made a concerted effort to swing his legs to the ground, clenching his jaw against the excruciating pain that must have followed.

"Gabriel, would you stop—"

"You're right. I can do it without pants." He ignored her attempts to push him back, yanking the IVs from his arms instead. The monitors started going crazy, but he ignored them too. "Just tell where he is. Is he still at Guilder?" His eyes flickered momentarily around the strange room. "For that matter...where are the hell are *we*, exactly?"

The questioned distracted him long enough that Rae was able to shove him unceremoniously back down on the bed—clutching at her own stitches all the while.

"You're not going anywhere, do you hear me?!" She was vaguely aware that she had to look absurdly non-threatening, waving a finger in a bathrobe, but she kept on anyway, "You just got shot, Alden. That may not mean anything to you, but it means something to me. Especially given the fact that..."

Her voice trailed off and he stared up at her—barely breathing.

When it became clear that she wasn't going to finish, he finally asked, "Especially given the fact that...*what?*"

Their eyes met in the darkness.

"Especially given the fact that your bullet was meant for me." A strange numbness was spreading out from the base of her skull and she felt like she was floating—watching herself have the conversation with Gabriel instead of actually participating. He was as riveted as her, eyes drifting in and out of focus as he struggled to remember. "You jumped in between me and the gun."

They were quiet for a long time.

A very long time.

So long, in fact, that Rae pulled the power cords out of the monitors before their frantic 'no-longer-attached-to-the-patient' beeping could drive them both mad.

"I remember that," Gabriel said at last, staring at the curtain, lost in thought. "I saw the guy take aim from the other side of the lawn. Saw you running to the Oratory."

He flinched as he recalled the moment of impact. They both flinched. Again, she took his hand. His eyes drifted down once more to the thin red line trailing down his chest, and this time, the significance of the event seemed to hit home.

"Did you make it?" he asked suddenly, his eyes snapping up to hers. "To the Oratory? And the rest of them..." he looked suddenly around, wondering if they were in beds next to his, "they made it out okay? Angel? Molly?"

"Everyone's fine," Rae assured him quickly, squeezing his fingers. "A couple broken bones, and Angel got hit over the head pretty bad—but she came out of it a few hours ago. The doctor says that she's going to make a full recovery. She's on the other side of the curtain." How she'd slept through the monitors and the noise they'd made was beyond Rae's comprehension. Or why none of the medical staff had come rushing in.

Gabriel's twinkling blue eyes were fixed on her now, except they weren't twinkling at all. In fact, his gaze was so intense and riveted, that for a minute, she remembered that she was talking to one of the most successful covert double-agents of all time.

"What doctor?" His voice was sharp as a knife. "Where are we?"

There was no backing out of it now...she'd just have to tell him. She only hoped that his newly repaired heart was up for the challenge. "Believe it or not, it all starts with Luke's dad..."

Rae and Gabriel talked together through the rest of the night. The initial story had taken long enough, and then there was a seemingly-endless aftermath to consider. Although his body may have been literally aching for rest, Gabriel's mind remained quick and alert, and every time she insisted they pick it up in the morning, he had staunchly refused, tugging her back down and forcing her to continue.

While he didn't know what to make of the Privy Council or Carter getting disavowed as president, he seemed just as mistrusting of the Knights as Devon was. And for that matter, just as intent upon putting Mallins in a shallow grave.

She tried to temper him as best he could, eyeing the heart monitor—the only one to have escaped his purge—nervously as his pulse both raced and slowed. But truth be told, the two of them were on exactly the same page. Laid raw by both the trauma of the attack and having the fundamental roots of everything they'd been counting on pulled out from under them. An endless series of raw nerves, fresh stitches, and short-tempered emotions all flying around. Not knowing where to settle or who to trust. Certainly, having no earthly idea what came next.

They were still going strong as the sun tinged the sky a morning shade of pink. If it hadn't been for the fact that Angel awoke with a shriek of joy upon seeing her brother when the curtain burst open, they would both most likely still be there lost in discussion.

As it stood, Rae had gone back to her bed to try and sleep for a few hours, and after having been cleared by Dr. Roscoe to venture forth into the world, she and her mother were taking an unexpectedly painful stroll through a small garden in the outer courtyard of the Knight's compound.

"How's it feeling?" Beth asked with concern, eying her daughter's tiny, unbalanced steps with a look of protection fit to rival Gabriel's.

Rae snapped out of her sleep-deprived trance and tried to give her mom a brave smile. "It's not so bad. Better than yesterday, for sure."

"Well, it would be even better than that if you hadn't snuck out both nights you were here for a midnight roundtable in the ICU." Beth shook her head disparagingly, but gave Rae's hand a little squeeze. "I'm so glad that he woke up, honey. I don't even know what I would've done."

"I know," Rae bit her lip and refused to let herself go there, "me too."

"How's he feeling? I went to check in on him before I came to get you, but he was asleep."

"He's..." how did one phrase it, "...vengeful?"

Beth chuckled. "I would imagine. Looks like both he and Angel weren't made to take a defeat like this in stride."

"A defeat?" Rae looked up at her in mild surprise. "Is that what you'd call this?"

Her mother's eyes turned thoughtful. "I don't know what to call this. All of you kids got out of there with your lives—for which I'm eternally grateful. But the evidence you went in to get..."

"...was basically destroyed."

Beth nodded. "And we're here, recovering at this wonderful facility, except..."

"...except this might be the very worst place in the world for us to be."

Beth's lips thinned into a hard line. "I never liked the Knights. They were a bit too moderate for my tastes. And I don't know what to think about Fodder. The man can be dangerous, that much has been proven in the past. He's also capable and intelligent—of that I'm certain. I'm just not sure if he can be smart."

"Smart?" Rae tripped forward a step and gripped onto her mother's arm. "What do you mean?"

"Right now, Andrew is in with both him and Angel. They're going over every piece of evidence there is in the world that Cromfield not only exists, but has been behind the bulk of criminal activity in the tatù world for the last several hundred years. They were able to get enough from the smashed hard-drive to corroborate with Angel's accounts, and together, I'd have to say the proof is pretty compelling. That's not the problem."

"The what is the problem?" Rae asked, navigating her way carefully across the stepping stones. There always seemed to be another issue or dilemma they would have to face. Would it ever stop?

Beth sighed. "The problem is that it's not something people *want* to believe. How do you fight against an enemy that's more myth than man? How do you defeat an immortal? I mean, as if his powers weren't bad enough, it's not like there's even a way to kill the guy—"

She stopped suddenly short as Rae froze beside her.

Immortality was a bit of a touchy subject these days. That combined with the fact that the only man destined to join her in the eternities was the one they were discussing...?

It was better not to touch on it at all.

"Honey," Beth backtracked quickly, "honey, I'm so sorry. I wasn't thinking—"

"It's okay," Rae said just as fast, clearing her face of all emotion. "It's a fact, isn't it? I'll have to deal with it sooner or later."

Beth gave her a long look, then squeezed her hand and forced a smile. "Well let's make it later, okay? Right now, I just want you to focus on making it around one more lap..."

Despite all the trouble she was having, Rae managed to scoff. "Please. Mom, I once scaled the outside of a fifty-foot granite building armed with nothing but a spandex jumpsuit and a piece of peppermint gum. I'm pretty sure I can handle one more lap—"

But just then, the ground slipped out from under her with a shrill, *yeep!*

Beth's arm flashed out to catch her, and she made a commendable effort not to roll her eyes. "That's right, sweetie. You're a regular hero. Not let's just try to keep you up on your own two feet..."

But Rae wasn't trying to stand on her feet. She wasn't trying to speak, or even looking about to see who might have seen her embarrassing spill. She had eyes for only one thing.

...and it was sparkling around her mother's finger.

"Mom," she said slowly, straightening herself up, "why are you wearing a ring?"

Beth flushed about a million shades of red in under a second. Her first instinct seemed to be to rip the thing off and hide it in her pocket, but one look at her daughter's face, and the jig was up. "Sweetheart," she looked just as out of sorts as Rae, "I wanted to wait for a better time to tell you. With everything that's been happening—"

*"Are you engaged?!"*

A group of passing Knights startled in alarm, and Beth flashed them a sweet smile before turning back to Rae. "Honey, this really isn't the time. You're still in the hospital, just out of bed, and to be honest, I kind of forgot I was wearing it, and—"

Rae looked up with tears in her eyes. "Carter asked you to marry him?"

Beth froze like a deer in the headlights, trying to interpret the tears. "About a week ago," she whispered. "Right after you left Scotland, actually."

Rae's jaw fell to the floor as she gawked at her mother's hand, pulling it closer for a better examination. "And you said...yes?"

It was a beautiful ring. There was absolutely no denying it. A stunning solitaire offset on all sides with tiny rubies—her mother's birthstone. The way the sun glinted off the crimson made the diamond itself look like it was almost on fire.

Rather fitting.

"Honey, let's just...let's just sit." Beth lowered her gently onto a nearby bench and turned so they were both facing each other. "I gave him a probationary yes."

There was a beat of silence.

"A *probationary yes*?" Rae exclaimed, torn between shock and laughter. "Is that even a real thing? What does that mean?" In an undertone, she added, "I don't think you can do that, Mom."

Beth's face remained gravely serious. "I would never make this kind of decision without talking with you first. We're a family, Rae. You and me. This needs to be a family decision."

Rae pulled back in surprise, genuinely touched. She had known for quite some time that Carter was in love with her mother. And lately, it had become hard to ignore the fact that her mother felt the same way. Their disgusting kisses were evidence enough of that. But she hadn't considered that marriage was ever on the table. And even if she had, she wouldn't have thought for a second that a decision like that would involve her. "Well..." she stalled, thinking fast, "if he makes you happy..."

Beth's eyes seemed to glow. "He makes me indescribably happy. I think he has for longer than I even realized..."

A thousand things danced through Rae's mind. A thousand different questions, and conflicts, and concerns. A thousand different untold possibilities that filled her with both excitement and dread. Andrew Carter as a step-father? Could the universe really be so strange?

But one look at her mother's radiant face silenced them all.

"In that case...when is the big day?"

Beth gave a high-pitched shriek and leapt upon her in a huge embrace completely forgetting the recent knife to the stomach. Rae bit her lip with a grimace, but hugged her back just as tight, a sea of happy tears spilling down her cheeks.

When they finally pulled away, Beth looked down at the ring for the first time, twisting it around thoughtfully with her fingers. "It's not going to be a big day. Both of us have lived full lives, we don't need all the fanfare now. Not to mention, this isn't the time, or place, or situation for it. We don't even know what Fodder and the Knights are going to decide to do..."

The soft sound of footsteps echoed from across the courtyard and Rae lifted her eyes in silent resignation.

"Well on that note...I think we're about to find out."

The two women looked up to see Carter, Devon, and Julian walked towards them, along with Fodder and about half a dozen of the Xavier guards. Before they could get close enough that Rae could even ask, Carter cleared his throat and stepped forward.

"Well, not only has Commander Fodder come to a decision regarding our situation with Cromfield, but he's decided to institute a plan as well." His eyes flickered to Fodder and he added in an undertone, "One which I can hardly condone."

Rae shifted nervously, so distracted that for a moment, she didn't even register the fact that she was talking to her future step-father. "Okay...what is it?"

Fodder stepped forward as well, standing shoulder to shoulder with Carter as he stared Rae down with the hint of a smile. "How would you feel about going back to your old school?"

# Chapter 5

"I said I got a real bad feeling about it, right?" Rae lifted her arms as best she could as Devon maneuvered a light sweater over her neck. As of last night, she had been officially discharged from the recovery wing and had been assigned a room in the residential barracks on the other side of the compound.

The 'compound' itself, turned out to be a lot bigger than she'd originally thought. It was well outside London, deep in the countryside in Surrey. Built to look like something vaguely resembling a monastery, it was divided into four parts: living quarters, training rooms, governmental chambers, and the hospital/mess. Although the facility itself was state-of-the-art, most people seemed to spend the bulk of their time outdoors, meeting and training in the endless courtyards and wide, fenced-off fields dotted along the rolling green hills. In a strange way, it actually reminded her a whole lot of Guilder...

Which brought her back to the problem at hand.

"I'm serious," she insisted, trying to stuff her palsied arms through the sleeves. "When Fodder said, 'how would you feel about going back to your old school,' I mentioned I thought it was a *terrible* idea, right?"

Devon chuckled softly, catching her flailing wrist and easing it through the hole. "You know we have to try."

"That's easy for you to say," she huffed. "You're not the one having a bit of PTSD here from your last alumni visit to campus..."

"And whose fault is that?" His eyes flashed, then cooled just as quickly. "Sorry," he muttered, as he continued to work.

Rae watched him in silence. Since she'd woken up a few days ago, they'd yet to discuss what had made him miss their fight with the Council in the first place. The huge blow-out they'd had when she found him collapsed in his apartment. Not to mention, his secret meetings with an Oxford scientist and a whole slew of other questionable behavior before that.

What with the 'near-dying' and all, they'd been too distracted to pay it much thought. A knife to her stomach had successful diverted their attention, and from the moment Rae had opened her eyes, they'd been too caught up in the euphoria of both being alive and in love to slow down for even a second.

But now that the IVs were out and people were waking up, now that she'd been transferred out of the hospital and into regular living quarters, their old problems were starting to circle back.

"And hey—everything turned out okay, didn't it?" he continued quickly, half-joking to lighten the mood. "Gabriel woke up. He was the last one. The final casualty."

"That's true...he woke up." Rae didn't think she would never get tired of saying those words. "And gave us his blessing, by the way."

Devon raised his eyebrows, looking interested. "Really?"

"Yep," Rae looked away as he knelt down to help her with her shoes, "said that we made a good fit."

No point in telling him about Gabriel's ambitious plan for an epic affair. The two already didn't like each other, and it would only throw fuel on the fire.

He straightened up in surprise, studying her speculatively. "Really?"

"Yes."

"Gabriel said that?"

"Yes."

"...*Really?*"

Rae cocked her hips impatiently. "*Yes.*"

Much to her surprise, a strange little grin was playing about his lips, accompanied by a calculating sort of mischief that made her nervous.

"Not that I even know what *us* is right now," she murmured, hurrying to change the subject, no matter the cost. "We haven't really gotten that far yet..."

Her voice trailed off and they both fell silent.

After a moment, Devon grabbed one of her scarves from inside the closet and began carefully winding it around her neck. His fingers grazed her skin as he swept up her hair, and she closed her eyes with a silent sigh.

No, they hadn't really gotten that far yet. Yet in some ways, they were closer now than they'd ever been before.

For the first time in their entire history, Devon had to care for her. Not just emotionally or logistically. Not by jumping off cliffs, or walking away from his family, or throwing himself into danger. But *physically*. He actually had to *physically* care for her.

She had never been hurt before. Not anything lasting, at least—not since she mimicked Charles' ability and learned how to heal. Okay, minus the time Kraigan had taken her healing tatù, but then she'd gotten it back again. She had never experienced the extreme vulnerability inherent in letting go of the reins and allowing someone else to take over.

And although she would rather have done it without the pain, there was an intimacy involved that she would have never imagined.

Last night, Devon had washed her hair. She had been trying to do it herself, of course. Stubbornly trying to lift her arms up over her head as the hot water beat down upon her. At one point, she cursed aloud in frustration. As usual, Devon heard her and came running.

At first she'd been embarrassed. No, embarrassed was too mild a word. *Mortified* was a better fit. Not only that she was physically unable to reach the tiny glob of shampoo she'd managed to fling up onto her scalp, but also by the fact that she was naked. And they were broken up.

Weren't they?

It was getting harder and harder to tell. If two people loved each other—deeply, profoundly loved each other—were they ever really broken up?

Two seconds after Devon joined her in the shower, she decided that she didn't care.

They didn't speak. Not the entire time. He simple offered her a tender smile, took off his clothes as well, and began working. His fingers combed gently through her hair, working the lavender soap up into a lather. When he was finished, he tilted her back into the water and rinsed it all clean even cupping his hand over her forehead so the water wouldn't get into her eyes.

There was no kissing. No ogling. No blushing faces or nervous looks.

There was just the two of them. As natural and perfect as could be.

Gabriel had said it well. They were a good fit.

Of course, that still didn't excuse anything.

"No," Devon said softly, looping the scarf one final time before he took a step away, "I guess we really haven't."

Rae bit her lip, wondering whether or not to proceed. "Now doesn't really seem like the best time to get into it..."

There was an entire Knights convoy headed to Guilder in about ten minutes. The Privy Council didn't know they were coming, and if their reception was anything like the last time, there was going to be hell to pay.

Devon sighed. "We could talk after...when we get back?" The idea was less than thrilling to the both of them. "Or we could do it now, if you want. I mean, we have a little—"

The door burst open and Molly stood framed in the doorway, her hair swishing out ahead of her with the momentum of her sudden half. "Rae, can I talk to you for a second? Alone? Hi, Devon," she added as an afterthought.

Devon shook his head and turned back to Rae with a faint smile. "Or maybe later?"

She forced herself to smile too. "Later it is. And thank you," she added, as he headed out the door, "for helping me get dressed."

Without stopping to think, he paced back across the room and kissed her square on the mouth. "I'll see you out there." Then he vanished through the door, leaving her confused and breathless in his wake.

Molly raised her eyebrows slightly as she pulled the door closed. "You two are kissing again? And he's helping you get dressed?"

"Yeah..." Rae tucked her hair behind her ears, "it's a little confusing."

Molly snorted. "Not as confusing as if he was helping you get *un*-dressed, I suppose."

"Funny." Rae shot her a playful glare as she gathered up her phone. "So what's up?"

Like flipping a switch, the gorgeous red-head grew suddenly grave. She cleared her throat, and with no preamble or context, abruptly announced: "I want to sell the penthouse."

Rae blinked, trying to figure out if she was serious. She certainly looked serious, only what the hell was she talking about?

"You want to sell the penthouse?" she repeated slowly.

"Yes, as soon as possible."

Rae shook her head. "I don't understand. We just bought it, barely lived in it, and now you want to sell it?"

Molly nodded. "Actually, you understand perfectly. That's exactly what I want to do."

"Okay, but where will we live then?"

"Well we can't live there anymore, can we?" She tossed her fiery hair back with a touch of frustration. "Everyone knows where it is—everyone who wants to kill us, that is—and so many terrible things have already happened in there, and there's simply no way to get that blood stain out of the Persian, and...and it's way too high up! What it all boils down to, is it's just no place to..."

Rae looked on incredulously. "It's no place to what?"

"I just don't want to live there anymore, okay?! We can't. And we need the money. So I want to sell it." She folded her hands in front of her as if the subject was closed. Then, in typical Molly fashion, she added, "So I put it on the market a few days ago."

*Of course she already put it on the market.*

Rae shook her head and tried to gather her thoughts. In a vague way, all those reasons made sense. The place had seen more calamity than several nuclear missile silos. But everything Molly was saying was kind of predicated upon the fact that whatever fight was coming next, they weren't going to be on the winning side. That, and her friend was clearly a manic nut-job.

Rae decided to handle the issues one at a time, starting with the most innocuous one first. "Okay, that's fine. I think I get everything you're saying. But don't you think you're taking this a little fast? I mean, look at where we are right now?" She gestured around them. "It's not exactly like we're in desperate need of money—"

"Of course we are," Molly snapped back with a passion that was a bit over the top, even for her. "It's time to grow up, Rae. We need to start thinking like adults. We can't just be...I don't know, buying up penthouses, then not living in them! It's..." Her face screwed up as she searched her vocabulary for the right word. "It's *fiscally irresponsible!*"

Rae burst out laughing. "Fiscally. Irresponsible. Two words I never, not in a million years, thought I'd hear coming out of your mouth. This is from the girl who shops at Sky Mall."

"Well, I'm turning over a new leaf, aren't I?" Molly bristled. "Not that you had much use for the penthouse anyway. You were always sneaking off to New York, or Scotland, or Devon's house...or Gabriel's place—"

"Hey!" Rae exclaimed. "Bit of a delicate subject, don't you think?"

Molly shrugged. "I'm just saying you're hardly going to notice it's gone."

"It's our *home*, Molly."

"Which you are hardly going to notice is gone."

Rae threw up her hands with an exasperated grimace. "Whatever. We can talk about it more in the car. Should be fun listening in for all the Knights riding with us." She held open the door, but Molly paused in the frame.

For a second, she peered frightfully down the hall—before she took a sudden step back into the room. "Actually...I think I'm going to sit this one out."

Rae stared at her in shock. In what world would Molly not be coming with them?

"Molls?"

But Molly was backing away now, shaking her head quickly back and forth and staring down the hall like at any moment, monsters might appear. "It's really dangerous and I just can't...I can't go back there."

*When the hell did something get 'too dangerous' for Molly Skye?!*

Rae let the door swing gently shut as she walked back towards her friend in concern. "Molls, is everything alright? Ever since we got back, you've been acting a little—"

"I just don't want to go, okay?" Molly shot back, flushing defensively. "The last time I was there I got a skull fracture, so pardon me if I don't want to go rushing back into danger. *Again*."

There was an anger in her voice that was fully justified, but it was what lurked just beneath the anger that had Rae so worried. It was fear. Pure unadulterated fear. The kind that she had never before seen in Molly. To be honest, she didn't think it was in her repertoire.

"Okay..." she said carefully, taking a little step back. "That's totally fine. I'll just..." As she glanced towards the window, a car honked in the drive. "I'll just see you when I get back?"

For a split second, a devastating look of indecision flashed across Molly's face. She actually took half a step towards Rae and the door, opening her mouth to speak, when something even stronger pulled her back. The next moment, it was like the whole thing never happened.

"Cool. Yeah, I'll see you when you get back." She folded her arms across her chest and glanced casually out the window, hiding her face. But as Rae headed out, Molly couldn't seem to help but add, "But be careful, Kerrigan. No more stabbings."

Rae flashed her a grin that didn't entirely hide her worry, and saluted. "No more stabbings." She should get that tattooed on her somewhere. Maybe right above the fairy...

The car was already packed by the time Rae got there. News of their previous little suicide mission to Guilder had spread quickly amongst the ranks of young Knights, and it seemed like everyone and their cousin was eager to prove themselves against the infamous Privy Council. Fortunately, most of these go-getters were confined to the training rings or compound patrols. But there were still several of them who had managed to con their way along. They watched Rae with narrowed, probing eyes as she walked past the large carrier truck and vans to slip into the one in the front.

Carter and Beth, Luke and his dad, and Devon were already waiting there. Julian had flat-out begged to go, but with a broken arm, he wasn't likely to be of much help if things went sideways.

"Where's Molly?" Devon asked as Rae climbed into the seat beside him. The second she was inside, the caravan shot off down the road.

Rae's eyes flickered to Luke, before she answered. "She's not coming."

Devon's eyebrows shot up, while Luke turned a worried face to the window.

"She's not coming?" Devon repeated incredulously. "What the hell does that even—"

"She said it's too dangerous," Rae replied, keeping her eyes fixed on Luke.

He must have felt her watching, but he seemed content to ignore her and stew in his own troubles, frowning out the window as they flew across the English countryside.

They drove in silence most of the way there. In fact, it wasn't until the Rae spotted the curved dome of the Oratory through the trees that Fodder finally leaned back to speak to her.

"The plan is simple," he said calmly. "We're going to take what's left of this hard-drive and present it to the upper members of the Council, along with our case. We'll leave them to punish Mallins however they see fit, but in the meantime, we'll be presenting a formal offer to join forces against this Cromfield. If he truly is as dangerous as you say, the sooner we strike the better. I don't want to wait for him to resurface and come out fighting—I want to make the first move."

Rae couldn't agree more. And in light of how many people of authority had let her down over the last few years, a part of her was thrilled to hear Fodder making the case for her. She nodded briskly hoping she looked professional while trying to ignore the flock of butterflies pounding away in her stomach the nearer they got to the gate. "And what would you like me to do? What would be the most helpful?"

Fodder gave her a shrew look, as if deciding whether her compliance was sincere. "I want you to stand right next to me and say nothing at all. Say nothing. Do nothing unless you're asked. I'll not have a repeat of your last Guilder encounter, Miss Kerrigan. These are peace talks. Nothing more. You will remain perfectly safe."

For the first time, Devon glanced at him with a hint of respect.

Rae, however, couldn't have been more confused. "Then...why exactly am I coming along? Most of the people in there hate me. They lump me in with my father and despise us both together. Aren't you afraid that just seeing me is going to set them off all over again?"

"They need to see you," Fodder countered. "Not only were you the one who uncovered Mallins' treachery and led the hunt to save the remaining hybrids, but from the sounds of it, Cromfield is specifically targeting you. You're not only his prime objective, but you remain the only one with the power and capacity to take him down. There is no fight without you, Miss Kerrigan."

*There is no fight without you.*

Rae's heart started racing as the rest of the world seemed to slow down. She didn't know why the words struck her so hard. She knew them to be true. Everyone around her knew them to be true as well. It was the fundamental basis upon which they'd derived countless plans. And yet, to hear a complete stranger say them. Someone with wisdom and clout. Someone with no personal stake in the matter other than he wanted to see his side survive...

There was something chilling about it.

"We're here!" the driver shouted back through the partition.

Devon squeezed Rae's hand as Carter and Beth stared fixedly out at the gate.

*Well, it's now or never.*

She cleared her throat and whispered, "Showtime."

"Commander Anthony Fodder of the Xavier Knights. I'm here to see President Mallins."

It was a testament to how the Kerrigan name was regarded in the world of tatùs that this statement had very little impact on the Guilder guard. He gawked openly through the window at Rae, jaw literally hanging ajar as he peered through the gates. They'd left the cars on the road, just walking to the gate seemed the better idea.

Fodder waited impatiently for a moment, before he rolled his eyes. "Yes, and that's Rae Kerrigan. We're both here to see Mallins. We harbor neither ill-will nor sinister intentions. We're only here to talk."

Devon growled under his breath, softer than anyone could hear. "Speak for yourself..."

"Only here to talk," the guard scoffed. "The last time she came to talk, the President ended up getting his face smashed in and half our agents were laid out cold."

Rae leaned forward indignantly. "In my defense, I never touched Mallins."

"No, that was all me." Devon smiled as he straightened.

"Enough," Fodder commanded. "Are you willing to open the gate? Or would you rather report to your commanding officer than when an envoy arrived from the Abbey?"

Rae shot Devon an inquisitive look and he murmured, "It's what the Knights call their headquarters."

Interesting. So she hadn't been all that off with the monastery reference after all.

With a rather spiteful look from the guard, the gate slid open with a judgmental creak. The trio of cars slipped quietly inside and parked next to each other in the lot. The air around literally crackled with tension as the group filed outside and started down the path to the Oratory. Or maybe it was actually the protective shield to keep out any unwanted tatùs.

Rae glanced nervously around. It felt as though the entire place was watching her. Like the trees themselves had eyes. In her imaginings, Madame Elpis was watching from the second story window the same way she had caught truants and kids breaking curfew for years. "I'm not going to lie," she said uneasily to no one in particular, "I'm feeling a really strong urge to become invisible right now."

One of the teenagers behind her glanced up in astonishment. "You can really do that?"

Devon ignored them, and slipped his arm around her with a chuckle. "Kind of defies the point of you being the 'symbol of reform' if no one can see you, right?"

Rae folded her arms across her chest and shivered. "I never wanted to be a symbol. Did I fail to make that clear? To strike it decisively *off* my list of things to do after graduation?"

Luke stepped between them with a smile. "Guys, this really isn't the time for—"

"Well Miss Kerrigan," The entire group stopped short as Victor Mallins walked out one of the doors from the two towers at the entrance. If he'd been at the Privy Council training facilities, he'd gotten here very quickly, unless he was speaking with the headmaster of Guilder Boarding School. Rae tried to remember if there were tunnels that led to the twin towers and came up short, she'd never noticed. She did notice, however, that Mallins was flanked by an entire platoon of guards.

"So Kerrigan, we meet again."

No, it was most definitely not the time for chitchat as Luke had just clarified.

In a clear demonstration of who was in charge, Commander Fodder stepped fearlessly forward—as impervious to the PC guards as he was undaunted by the President.

Rae wondered why the PC President had been such a secret when it seemed everyone knew. Hadn't that been a huge issue the year Kraigan had come? Maybe he had been trying to show her it wasn't as big of a secret as everyone thought back then. My, how times had changed. Rae blinked and focused back on what Fodder was saying.

"Mr. Mallins. You're looking well."

There was a tittering amongst the Knights.

Mallins did not look well. He did not look well at all. In fact, if Rae hadn't known the person who had nearly beat him to death personally, she would have wondered what in the name of heaven or hell could have done such a thing.

His eyes and mouth were swollen with some dark discoloration near his jaw where Devon had dislodged it from the rest of his skull. The remainder of his skin was a sickly shade of bruised yellow, and there was a thick cut across the bridge of his nose just like Julian had.

His mouth twisted into a crooked line when Fodder spoke, but he remained as calm and collected as ever. "Mr. Fodder." Rae noticed that neither man consented to address the other by their title. She wondered whether this would have been different if Carter was still in charge. "Once again, you come by unannounced. And carting this girl." His eyes narrowed as they landed once more on Rae. "Tell me, why are you here? I beg you to keep it brief as I'm afraid the patience of the Council for such antics has been recently stretched rather thin."

Fodder looked him square in the eye. "Actually, if it's all the same to you, I'd rather speak to someone who will still be representing the Council this time tomorrow. A lieutenant, perhaps?"

The space around them suddenly went very still.

Mallins eyes seemed to glow with sheer loathing. "Is that a threat?"

Fodder smiled. "More of a hunch. You see, Victor, after stabbing Miss Kerrigan in the stomach, you did your very best to destroy the evidence she'd come that day to collect." He held out his hand and an agent behind him handed him the remains of the disk. "But you didn't get all of it."

Mallins zeroed in on the damaged device, but he showed no fear. "And what, pray tell, is that?"

*Say nothing. Do nothing. Act like you're not even there.*

But Rae had never been that great at following orders...

"It's proof that you used the sanctity of the Privy Council to conduct fatal experiments on hybrids, just like my father did," she growled. "It's evidence that you tarnished Guilder's name with the blood of countless men, women, and children—all of whom you conveniently *disappeared*."

When she was finished with the little speech, she shrank back into the crowd, feeling Fodder's disapproving eyes on her the entire time.

The words had done the trick, however, because about half of the guards positioned around Mallins were staring at him in shock. The word of a Kerrigan alone wouldn't have been enough to sway them, but many of them knew Rae personally. Some of them had even worked together. And despite the cognitive dissonance it entailed, at some point or another, all of them had heard the rumors of people being disappeared.

Mallins' eyes never left her face. "What an inventive story you've created. Sociopathic lies must run in the family."

Beth's hands glowed with blue flames, but Carter squeezed her wrist in caution.

With a look of supreme disdain, Fodder tossed the drive to Louis Keene—the second in command, a man who had been promoted heavily despite his relatively young age. It was a brilliant move. Keene's youth meant that he couldn't have possibly been at Guilder to be complicit in the crimes.

"Do with that what you like. Who runs this Council is of no concern to me." He lowered his voice intently. "We've come today for a different reason."

The PC agents shifted nervously, many of them casting distressed looks at Rae and Devon. She could practically feel him aching to reach out to them by her side, but for once, his true loyalty didn't lie to the Council itself. It lay with the cause.

"Oh yes?" Mallins snapped. "And what's that?"

"We've come to extend a hand of allegiance. An offer to combine forces in order to defeat a man more villain than even yourself. Jonathon Cromfield."

This time, the surprise in the ranks of the Council agents was much more pronounced. Some of them were staring at Fodder like they'd like to rip his head off, but many more were casting similar looks of distrust towards Mallins.

Rae folded her arms across her chest with a smirk.

Mallins may have weaseled his way in to the presidency, but he had one great thing working against him. No matter what may have happened recently to dislodge him—the people of Guilder *loved* Carter. He was widely regarded as one of the greatest Presidents and Headmasters the Council and the school had ever seen. The fact that he was standing beside the Knights spoke volumes.

Volumes that even Mallins would have a difficult time trying to control.

"Give it up, Victor," Rae murmured, "it's the only move and you know it. We're going to need all our strength to fight this enemy."

But the old man was not to be taken down so easily.

"Oh Miss Kerrigan," his face wrinkled up into a cracked smile, "the only enemy I see standing before us... is you."

# Chapter 6

Julian was waiting for them by the Xavier Knight's gate. Rae shouldn't have been surprised. The second Mallins heard they were at the Guilder, she figured Julian saw him decide what he was going to do. She was surprised he hadn't just called and told them to come back. Not to waste their time.

One arm came up in a half-hearted wave, as the line of cars filed gloomily past into the compound. The other was still fastened across his chest in a sling. The second they were parked, Rae jumped from the car and walked straight towards him.

There had been no talking on the way back. Not a single word, and the trip was over an hour long. It was claustrophobic as hell. Despite the high leather ceiling inside, and the wide open hills outside, Rae felt like she might smother.

"Nice visit, huh?" Julian asked sarcastically, wrapping his good arm around her and leading her away from the group of stoic Knights. Devon looked like he wanted to come with them, but the second he'd set foot on the gravel driveway, Carter and Beth had pulled him aside for a hurried talk.

Rae blew her hair out of her face and shook her head. "Why didn't you text me? I could've turned us around at Guilder's gates."

Julian's dark eyes softened sympathetically. "I wanted to, but I don't think the meeting was as black and white as you think."

"What does that mean?"

He opened his mouth to answer, but they both fell silent as the same group of angry looking young Knights stormed past— sending up frustrated sprays of gravel in their wake. The two friends waited until they were clearly out of earshot before resuming their conversation.

"It means, Mallins wasn't the only one at the meeting."

Rae considered that for a moment, and for the first time since that morning, a little flutter of hope stirred in the pit of her stomach. "You're talking about Keene? The second in command?"

Julian nodded. "Keene and others. It was a powerful visual, to see Carter standing with the leader of the Knights. People miss him there. The agents as well as the staff. And Keene is a good man. They might be willing to listen to what he has to say."

"Well that may be true, but Guilder is on virtual lockdown. Devon told me that they're even revoking student privileges into town. How the hell are we going to figure out who's with us and who's on the other side?"

There was a pause, and Julian's already bruised face darkened with frustration. "I haven't worked that part out yet."

At that moment, Fodder waved the two of them over and their shoulders fell with a sigh.

"Is he really angry with me?" Rae whispered nervously. "He told me not to say anything, but I couldn't help myself. Maybe I made things worse?"

When Julian didn't say anything, she tugged impatiently on his sleeve.

"Jules?"

He glanced down. "Oh, that wasn't rhetorical? I read futures, Rae—not emotions. Have you been getting that wrong all this time?"

Despite the present mood, she shoved him playfully a few steps away. "Smart ass."

"Good, Julian, you're here too," Fodder said as soon as they arrived. "We're holding an emergency meeting in the bunker. Join us."

Rae fell into automatic step behind him, but Julian paused. A muscle in the back of his jaw flexed as he stared intently into the Commander's eyes.

"Is that an order?" he asked quietly.

Fodder pulled himself up to his full height, staring the teenager down with a gravitas that sent chills running down the back of Rae's spine. Julian, however, was undaunted. He simply stared evenly back, the cuts and bruises on his face making him look years older than he was.

"It's an invitation," Fodder said sharply, although his tone implied otherwise.

It looked like Julian was about to refuse, but luckily at that moment, Carter and Beth walked forward with Devon trailing a few steps behind. Carter took one look at the standoff and clapped Julian gently on his uninjured shoulder.

"Come on, Julian. Walk with me."

Julian turned his back on the Commander and obeyed his old President without a moment's pause. Several scattered Knights around the courtyard were discreetly watching the whole thing with rather murderous expressions. Expressions that only darkened as Devon flashed them a look of equal loathing and fell in step behind Carter.

Rae stood frozen in place, unsure what to do.

Of course she knew the Knights and the Council had a volatile history. One full of sabotage, conflicting doctrines, and at times, brutal retaliation. But any open hostilities had cooled over a decade ago. Before she even got to Guilder or found out about her tatù. It had been a Cold War since then, but one that had little consequence on the real world. Lately, the two organizations merely spied on each other and deliberately paid the other no mind. They existed in two completely separate orbits. Ones that both sides took great care to ensure never intertwined.

Until now.

The soft hum of angry voices sounded from the other side of the courtyard, and Rae suddenly wished that she wasn't able to so perfectly hear. Looked like the Cold War had heated up by several thousand degrees. And the timing couldn't be worse.

She winced apologetically at Fodder, but he didn't look in the least bit put out. In fact, if she didn't know better, she'd have to say that a part of him admired Julian for his defiant loyalty.

Then again, now was not the time for such partisan politics. They had to unite, or they would fall. There was no third option.

He raised his hand and gestured inside. "Shall we?"

Her eyes flashed cautiously to his group of disgruntled followers, but she nodded her head.

"We shall."

The 'bunker' was actually set up to look almost identical to the Council's 'situation room.' A large map with blinking dots was pressed against the far wall lit up with coordinates, tiny faces, and scribbles of writing in every language imaginable. There was a long oval table in the middle with the same wheeled chairs Rae and Molly had once been reprimanded for spinning on during a debriefing, and along the walls was mounted the exact same curved shelving—groaning under the weight of countless manila files.

"Well, the Privy Council and the Xavier Knights have at least one thing in common," she whispered to Devon as they filed quietly inside.

"Besides a shared hatred for us?"

"Okay, two things. I was going to say a decorator."

His eyes flickered casually around the room, but Rae knew that he was soaking in every relevant detail, committing them all to memory. But no sooner had he started, then a member of the Knights reached below the table and hit a hidden switch. All at once, the blinking lights and writing on the map disappeared, leaving a blank canvas in their wake. He caught Devon's eye from across the room, and Devon smiled sweetly before settling himself into a chair.

"So untrusting..." he murmured, with a faint smirk.

Rae rolled her eyes. "Look who's talking. Is that a knife in your jacket pocket?" She recognized the faint outline.

"Don't be silly, Rae. They confiscated all of our weapons when we came in here." He leaned back in his chair. "I had to make my own."

He was spared her admonishment, because at that moment, Fodder pounded a small gavel against the table to begin the meeting.

Rae and Devon's eyes locked at once upon the medieval-looking hammer.

*A gavel? Really?*

"First of all, I wanted to thank you all for being here," Fodder began diplomatically. "I realize we've been brought together under a rather strange set of circumstances, and while some of us are still recovering, I appreciate the effort being made by the rest." His eyes flickered over Julian and Devon, who both stubbornly returned his gaze. "As for the meeting this morning with the Privy Council, I would have to say the whole thing was a tremendous success."

*I'm sorry. Did he say...success?*

Rae leaned forward in her chair, staring towards the front of the table. Fodder didn't appear to be joking. Neither, for that matter, did Carter who was seated by his side. The rest of the table was in a similar state of confusion to hers, but none of the Knights appeared willing to question their leader.

The PC agents showed less restraint.

"What the hell is that supposed to mean?"

Rae heard the words coming out of her mouth before she made the conscious effort to say them. It was the outburst with

Mallins all over again, but this was too big an issue to just let hang.

A success?! Were they talking about the same meeting?!

Fodder turned to Carter with a low undertone. "She does that a lot, doesn't she?"

Carter shook his head. "You have no idea."

"I'm sorry," Rae continued, sounding not sorry at all, "but in what possible dimension could you ever call that meeting a success? They threw us out of the school. Not a single person either spoke up for us, or went with us when we left. The entire thing was a total catastrophe!"

"The point of the meeting was not to acquire Guilder support."

Rae's eyes shot from Fodder to Carter, sure she had heard wrong. She wasn't the only one.

Both Devon and the greasy blond-haired instigator she had heard bad-mouthing them in the halls spoke up at the same time.

"Then what was it?"

They flashed each other twin looks of malice, before turning their eyes front.

"Andrew," Fodder gestured to the table, "would you care to do the honors?"

He was a statesman, through and through. Rae had been in enough high-power political situations (most recently with the royal family) to recognize it at once. Although the table was evenly divided—PC on one side and Knights on the other—the two men had pushed their chairs together at the head. Demonstrating clear, equal leadership. And although they were technically in the Knights territory, Fodder was giving Carter the opportunity to essentially run the meeting.

She had to respect it. Even if she didn't quite trust it. It demanded respect.

"Thank you, Anthony." Carter got to his feet. "The point of the meeting was to cement the alliance of the people gathered together in *this* room."

"But..." Rae looked from one to the other, "I thought the Knights were already with us against Cromfield. I thought they were going to—"

"We were, by no means, *with you*, Miss Kerrigan," Fodder interrupted. "We got a call from my son saying that the Privy Council's top agents were about to be executed for insubordination on Guilder grounds? Yes, that warrants a rescue attempt. If the intelligence gathering opportunities weren't enough, we would have done it just for your age. But when you told me that you were there trying to prove that your own Council had been corrupted, so that you could gather support to fight against a man the entire world believes to be dead? No. Miss Kerrigan. That required a bit more proof than Miss Cross' stories, and your collective promise."

A surge of anger welled up inside Rae's chest, but at the same time, she realized that everything he was saying was perfectly justified. If she had been in his place, in charge of a large group of generally young people, and had been told to send them into the flames based on their word of her sworn enemies? No. She probably wouldn't have done it either.

*And who was Miss Cross? Oh, Angel!* "So why did we go to Guilder?" she asked again. "Why didn't you just turn us loose—"

"Because the only way I was going to believe it was true, was if I heard it from Mallins' own mouth," Fodder concluded. "Which, I'm pleased to say, I did."

Before Rae could even ask, a tiny dark-haired boy stepped forward from the shadows behind Fodder's chair. He was so slight, he seemed to just blend in with the room around him. But when Fodder gestured him forward, he stepped eagerly into the light.

"This is Kyo," Fodder explained. "He's been with the agency now for about two years."

*So what...since he was nine?*

"I'm seventeen," Kyo blurted, correctly interpreting the baffled looks from the PC.

Rae couldn't help but grin. This was a kid who was used to getting underestimated. She knew the feeling well. And she wouldn't do it for one second.

"Kyo came to us with a very special gift," Fodder offered the child a rare smile, "he has the innate ability to tell when people are lying, or telling the truth."

*Boy would that come in handy!*

Rae eyed the child speculatively, wondering if she'd be able to get close enough for an opportunistic hug. On her other side, Devon seemed to be wondering the same thing—brow creasing with a worried frown as he angled himself between the two.

*Yeah...I bet that's one gift you hope I never have.*

But something about Fodder's story didn't add up.

"I don't understand," Rae said in confusion, "wouldn't he have had to have been there? To see Mallins in person?"

"He was there." Fodder placed a hand on the boy's back. "You just weren't able to see him."

The next second, it was like Kyo was never there.

Every member of the PC sat up in alarm, muscles tensed at high alert as their gifts and senses ranged out to find him. Julian's eyes flashed momentarily white, Beth's hands flamed blue, while Devon got that dilated look of focus he did whenever he was listening very hard.

Rae was the only one who seemed completely delighted. Kyo's power wasn't quite like her invisibility—it was more like a camouflage. Actually, it was a great deal like Kraigan's in that regard, slippery little sucker. But it wasn't the power itself that had her smiling.

It was the fact that the kid had two.

When he popped back into focus, he was right by her side. The half of the table who had never seen his trick before gasped in shock, but he and Rae shared a little grin. Then, before any one of the Knights could stop him, he held out his little hand.

"Want to share?"

Rae didn't think there was a sweeter way he could have asked. Her eyes flickered up to Fodder, asking silently for permission, and the man bowed his head. Then, with a feeling of great anticipation, she reached out and wrapped her fingers around the boy's wrists.

Hybrid powers felt nothing like the rest. Even though she was braced for it, Rae found that she was hardly prepared. Her neck curved down to her chest with a little gasp as she felt the full force of it running through her veins. There was the truth aspect—hovering just a little below the surface—just begging to be used. The camouflage was predictably a little harder to locate, but she knew she would be able to develop it in time. Hybrid powers always took longer for her to master. She was still up to her ears trying to figure out Ellie's and that had been over a year ago.

"Are you really sure you wanted her to do that?"

Rae looked up in surprise to see the greasy-haired boy at it again. He was staring up at Fodder with a great deal of respect, and yet, harsh dislike twisted the rest of his features.

Fodder gave him a sharp look. "Miss Kerrigan is our guest, Drake. She's welcome to share in any tatù. As long as its owner gives her consent," he added pointedly, casting Rae a warning look.

She nodded respectfully, still marveling in the complexity of Kyo's ink.

"So you knew Mallins was lying," Beth summarized, bringing them back on point. "And not just about himself, but about Cromfield as well."

Fodder nodded. "Sometimes it's better to judge a man by the things he neglects to say, rather than by the things he says out loud. Mallins said nothing to deny any charges, but the truth was written all over his face. After being further assured by Kyo, I am convinced. And therefore, the Knights are convinced as well."

He shared a quick glance with Carter, who nodded slowly.

"The Xavier Knights will help you in this quest to defeat Cromfield. It would seem that it's in all of our best interest to do so, as the man has designs not only for Miss Kerrigan, but for the rest of the tatù world."

Carter cleared his throat and stepped forward. "We're only being given one advantage in this fight, and it's a slight advantage at that. *Time*. We have been told by reliable sources that it was Cromfield's intention to go 'underground,' so to speak. With all three of his chief lieutenants out of the picture, I imagine he's looking for time to regroup. This window of opportunity is the only chance we'll get to gather our forces together and make an assault."

"It won't be easy," Fodder picked up right where Carter left off. "Since the Privy Council is obviously refusing to acknowledge the problem, it seems we'll be on our own. We're going to have to put every effort forward if there's even a chance this is going to work. Training schedules are being increased tenfold. Any non-essential or non-tatù'd personal will be on recon—searching for any and all rogue operatives in the field that could help us."

His eyes seemed to glow as he stared down both sides of the table.

"This is a battle where every single person counts. I will not have our chances be diminished by petty in-fighting or pre-conceived prejudices. If this man and myself," he gestured to Carter, "can see past our differences and come together, then there is no reason in the world why that wouldn't apply to the rest of you. Refusal to comply with this alliance will quite simply not be tolerated."

He got to his feet and it was clear the meeting had come to an end. An aide pulled open the door in front of him, but before he walked through, he turned back with one final message.

"We're in this together now. Understand that. Our fates are tied together and we are dependent upon the unit as a whole."

The glaring line separating both sides of the table suddenly couldn't have been more obvious.

"Make me proud."

"So we're all on the same team now?" Gabriel sat up as straight as he could on the infirmary bed, ignoring the searing pain that followed. "What are we? Council or Knights?"

"I think that was Fodder's point," Julian answered, "we're both. I mean—neither. I mean...I don't know." He pulled his dark hair back into a ponytail with a sigh. "We're going to have to come up with some sort of new name."

"We could be the Cights?" Molly offered hopefully. "Or the Knouncil."

Rae bit her lip, while the rest of them shook their heads with various levels of rebuke.

"It's probably best if we don't try to combine them, babe." Luke squeezed her hand.

"Whatever." Molly had a notoriously short temper these days. "So what exactly are the lot of us supposed to do? Make anti-Cromfield banners?"

Devon's eyes flickered out the ICU window, where a large group of teenage Knights was going through their daily training routine. "We're supposed to train with them."

A charged quiet settled over the little room.

"Well I think that sounds great." Gabriel was predictably onboard. "Any opportunity to kick the ass of a Xavier Knight is fine by me."

Even Devon perked up at that, and he and Julian shared a grin.

"I'd be down..." Angel cocked her head to the side, also staring at Julian, "if you are."

As had become his custom, Julian's eyes flashed automatically white before they cleared back to the present.

"It's what Carter wants," he said quietly, glancing at Rae to see her reaction. "And I hate to say it, but Fodder's right. This fight with Cromfield is coming, and since we burned the bridge with the PC, we don't have anyone to help us fight it. An alliance with the Knights seems like the only play left on the board."

Rae stared out the window and bit her lip. "A lot of them are going to get hurt," she murmured, almost to herself. "They haven't been through what we've been through; they have no idea what they're going to be up against."

"Who cares?" Gabriel asked callously. "You know they wouldn't care if it was us."

An echo of the conversation she'd overheard between the Knights in the corridor flashed through Rae's mind. No, some of them certainly wouldn't care. Then she thought of the girl. But some of them would...

"We need to be better than that," she said firmly. "Yeah, Cromfield is a fight that belongs to us all, but it started with the people right here in this room. And I have a sinking feeling that no matter what happens it's going to come down to the people right here in this room as well. We're not going to be nameless faces to Cromfield. It's personal with us. And he knows it. It's personal with him, too."

Her eyes flicked from Molly and Luke—sitting far more on the periphery than was custom, to Devon—still watching the Knights training, to Julian—searching aimlessly through the future, and finally to Angel and Gabriel—the closest thing to children that Cromfield had.

Yes, it was going to be personal to him. But it was personal to her, too.

The fight that was coming was an equal match of wills. An equal level of hurt, and an equal level of terrifying devastation that was sure to follow.

Knights or Council. Friends or foes. Alliance or not.

In the end, it was just her and him.

There would be no last one standing.

They'd just have to see who came out on top.

# Chapter 7

"Come on, Drake! Let her have it!"

Rae and her friends watched silently as their greasy-haired nemesis threw tiny smoking fireballs at the girl who had defended them earlier in the hall. She was doing rather well, protecting herself with what looked to be some kind of force-field, but he was still advancing. In the end, she fell back a step under the weight of the blast and raised her hands in surrender. Drake spun back around to the applause of the Knights, a rather devious look in his eye.

The only people not applauding were the small group of PC teenagers sitting on a picnic table in the shade. Even Gabriel had been allowed out of the ICU to observe, and sat lounging with the rest of them, taking careful mental notes on their opponents.

Or their allies.

Or...whatever they were supposed to call them.

They looked good. Really good. Rae had to admit it. While their powers might not be as developed as any Guilder student's would have been by that age, they were in prime fighting form and, for the most part, their technique was commendable. Yep, they looked good. Certainly better than how Rae and her friends appeared right now.

While she was dressed in regular training clothes, head to toe black, a roll of tight-fitting bandages lay wrapped bracingly around her stomach, making it a bit hard to move and kind of a pain in the butt to take a deep breath. Julian's arm hung still fastened across his chest in a sling, Angel had a single piece of black gauze wrapped around her head like a pirate, and Gabriel had thrown caution to the wind, leaning casually back against the picnic table with no shirt and only a pair of loose-fitting scrubs. There was a huge bandage taped across his chest where he'd gotten shot, and just from taking the brief walk from the ICU to the grounds, small stains of blood were already leaking through. He acted oblivious to it, but it had to hurt.

No, the ex-agents of the PC didn't look like much no matter what their files might say. But there wasn't a shadow of a doubt in Rae's mind that every single one of them could take down any of the Knights standing before them.

They were better. That's all there was to it. They were in a whole other league.

"How about it, Guilder?" Drake-the-obnoxious called over his shoulder, smirking tauntingly at the table. "Got anything that could beat that?"

Angel sighed loudly, turning to her friends. "Don't make it worse for him, you guys. You know what they say: tiny fireballs, tiny—"

"Yo, Barbie! You want to say that to my face?"

It was a testament to the total lack of fear each of the 'Guilders' felt that this challenge was met with a soft chorus of laughter. Rae knew they all had similar thoughts running through their heads. They had all called Angel 'Barbie' at one point or another. Her adopted brother made it a point to call her it at least once a day. But no matter how delicate Angel might look, she could mop the field with this guy if she wanted to. Massive head wound or not.

Drake paced forward, enraged by the lack of opposition. Two men and a girl followed along behind, flanking him on either side.

"I said," he growled through his teeth, "say that to my face."

At this point, Julian and Gabriel stopped smiling.

"Take a step back," Julian said softly. "No one here wants to see you get hurt."

This time it was Drake who laughed. "And who's going to hurt me? You? What're you going to do? Tell me my fortune? Nice arm, by the way."

Julian's dark eyes fixed on him intently. Behind his back, Devon leaned causally forward, every muscle in his body at attention.

Julian didn't even blink as he stared steadily at the cocky idiot in front of him. "No, I wasn't talking about me. If I were you, I'd be far more worried about my girlfriend. She's been known to have a bit of a temper..."

Angel smiled sweetly, and despite his bravado Drake shuddered and took a step back, and then another.

That should've been the end of it. The situation should've been successfully diffused.

Until a Knight at the back of the field called to Drake with a sly look in his eye. "Really, man? You're just going to let that go? You're going to be talked out of it by the broken guy with the Barbie girlfriend?" the guy scoffed. "If I was you, I'd *do something about it.*"

The final words seemed to almost echo in the open air, and the next thing Rae knew Drake was thundering back across the field making a bee-line for their table.

Except, he never got there.

At first, Rae didn't know what was happening. She glanced around wildly, trying to figure it out.

Drake stopped mid-step, freezing in place like he'd walked straight into a wall. It looked exactly like Angel's freezing power, except, she needed to touch someone to do that and she hadn't moved from her seat at the table.

Angel was, however, the only one who didn't look surprised. She looked concerned instead. "Gabriel," she said quietly.

The rest of the table turned to Gabriel, in shock. At first glance, he didn't appear to have moved either. He was staring at Drake like the rest of them, his head tilted slightly to the side.

Then Rae caught him lifting two fingers.

"*Gabriel*," Angel said again, a little more forcefully this time.

But Gabriel didn't move. He just stared at the frozen boy with a hard smile that didn't quite reach his eyes. "Bet you don't have a lot of information on me, do you, *boy*? No file?" he asked casually, completely immune to the tension around him. A few yards away, Drake's face had begun to turn blue. "Metal manipulation. That's what I am down on paper if there is a file." A little smirk turned up the corners of his lips as he leaned forward. "Of course...no one ever realizes exactly what that means."

All at once, Drake's face twisted in absolute agony. There was a tortured cry, and the next second he fell to his knees.

Angel was on her feet at once, standing in between them. "Gabriel, stop it *now*," she growled through her teeth.

With a look of supreme unconcern, Gabriel lifted his fingers and released Drake. It was like cutting a puppet's strings. Drake's entire body shut down as he fell onto the grass with a piercing cry. A dozen or so of his friends rushed forward to surround him, but Rae and her group only had eyes for Gabriel.

And Gabriel only had glaring eyes for Drake.

"How did—" Drake sputtered and trembled, wrapping his arms around himself as he was lifted to his feet. "What did you do to—?"

"Ever wonder how much iron a person has in their blood?" Gabriel interrupted calmly.

His face was a mask of indifference, but Rae was horrified. On either side of her, Julian and Devon were staring at Gabriel like they'd never seen him before. In a way, they hadn't. They'd certainly had no idea he could do something like this.

Gabriel ignored them completely, keeping his eyes locked on Drake. "I don't need to leave my seat to kill you. I don't need to do anything more than lift a finger to reverse the flow of blood to your heart, which, I've heard, is a particularly painful way to go."

There was fire in his eyes now. A lethal look of promise that darkened the sunny day. "Every person at this table could kill you in two seconds flat. So my advice, kid, is this..." He leaned forward, sending a collective shiver through the Knights. "Don't give them a reason to."

"What the hell is going on here??"

There was a loud bang as the door to the outer courtyard opened and shut. Fodder moved quickly across the grass, followed closely by Carter. Fodder's eyes flickered immediately from Gabriel's casually threatening posture, to his fallen agent, then back to the bullet hole in Gabriel's chest.

One of them seemed to negate the other, and he hesitated, unwilling to accuse.

Carter didn't appear to have the same problem.

"Alden! What did you do?"

Gabriel stared unabashedly up from the picnic bench, but before he could say anything that was sure to land him in a heap of trouble, a voice piped up from the back of the Knights.

It was the same girl Rae had heard defending them in the hall, the same one who'd fallen prey to Drake and his impotent fireballs. "It wasn't his fault," she said quickly. "It was Eeks'."

*Eeks?* Rae glanced quickly at her friends. *Who the hell was Eeks?*

But strangely enough, the rest of the Knights fell instantly in line with this accusation, and they turned around as one, staring at the boy who'd spoken up from the back. His face flushed guiltily and Rae remembered the strange way his words had fallen on the air. Maybe there had been more to them than met the eye?

"Power of persuasion," Fodder said softly to Carter. "If he wants something done, he needs only suggest it." He raised his voice and called across the grass. "Mr. Benjamin Eeks, is this true?"

Benjamin pawed nervously at the ground. He shifted nervously from side to side before muttering, "Yes, sir."

"Laps." Fodder didn't even look at him when he said the word. He and Carter simply turned around and started walking back to the compound. When they were halfway there, Fodder paused. "The rest of you, continue training. If I have to come out here again, you can all join Mr. Eeks. I don't care who started it." His eyes rested briefly on Gabriel. "Or what condition you're in."

Benjamin set out in a quick jog around the compound as Fodder and Carter disappeared inside.

Once they were gone, Rae turned to Gabriel accusingly. "What the hell were you thinking?" she hissed. "You could've killed him!"

"That's exactly what I want *him* to think," Gabriel shot back. "That I *could* have killed him. We all could. But we didn't."

She shook her head, watching as Drake was half-carried back into the ranks. "I don't think that distinction is going to mean a whole lot to him."

Gabriel followed her gaze with an almost critical stare. "I believe it's the only thing that will."

When they left an hour later, Eeks was still running.

"Did you have any idea that Gabriel could do that?" Rae asked later that night.

She was pacing manically around her room, conjuring random items and stuffing them in drawers and along the shelves to make the place feel more like home. Devon was perched in the middle of the bed, watching her.

"No, I didn't," he answered softly. "And that alone is scary as hell. Makes me wonder if he was saving it for something..."

Rae paused, thrown by his assessment. "What? You think he was going to use it on you in the dead of night? I told you, Dev, he gave us his blessing."

Devon shook his head with a faint grin. "Okay, first of all—that's absolute bullshit. I don't care what the guy says. He wants you. He always will. So that means he'll always hate the idea of you and me. There's no way he's giving it his *blessing*."

"Then why would—"

"Because that's what guys do, Rae. We act like we're okay with things, but we're not."

Rae rolled her eyes. "Well, that's rather passive aggressive of you." Why was part of her just the teeniest bit glad that Gabriel wanted her? She shook off the thought. "What's the second thing?"

"The second thing is—I wasn't talking about him saving it for me. It's more like..." he paused uncertainly, wondering how to phrase it, "he and Angel have way more damage than the rest of us. Which sometimes seems impossible, I know, but it's true. They grew up with Cromfield as their teacher, mentor, and father figure. There's a lot they've been through that we've no idea about."

Rae sat down on the edge of the bed, staring at him curiously. "I get that. They were basically bottle-fed by Cromfield. What do you expect from them?"

"Nothing," Devon said quickly. "I think the fact that they were able to get themselves through something like that and come out even remotely normal on the other side is a testament to their character—all by itself. That's not what I meant."

"Then—"

"I'm only saying...they can't erase everything. You know?"

Unfortunately, Rae did know. The adopted siblings had a whole litany of strange and often dark quirks that were constantly presenting themselves. For example, Angel was turning out to be a bit of a kleptomaniac. It didn't matter that she had money for anything she could want, or that she had a friend who could conjure her anything she couldn't find; she delighted in the thrill of occasional thievery. Julian had confessed that she'd shoplifted him a candy bar on their first date together. At the time, it had seemed unconventionally charming—a kid who had grown up stealing things she needed to survive swiped him a token at the movies. But as the months progressed, shoplifting turned out to be the least of their problems.

Angel slept with the lights on. When no one was around to call him on it, Gabriel did, too. It was impossible to catch either of them at a moment when they weren't armed, and they were the kind of people who shot first and asked questions later. They were slow to trust, and even slower to act on that trust. Rae knew; she understood some of it, sympathized for their past, but also stayed partially prepared for them to surprise her.

It was the psychological damage Devon was talking about. The moral compass inside them that—no matter what they did to change it—was always tilting slightly to the left.

"I would never have done what Gabriel did," Devon said quietly. "I certainly wouldn't have done it just to prove a point. He's lucky nothing went wrong. That guy could have been seriously hurt. I don't care if he deserved it or not. We just...don't *do* that."

Rae sighed, pushing her long hair up out of her face.

Devon was right. No matter how many times the game was explained to them, both Angel and Gabriel played by a slightly different set of rules.

"Angel stopped him," she offered half-heartedly.

Devon gave her a sarcastic look. "After the kid was already on the ground. And you know she only did that because Jules was there. She always tries harder when he's around."

"So what do you suggest?" Rae asked briskly, eager to move on. She'd spent countless nights worrying about exactly this problem, and she was sure she'd spend countless more. She didn't want to dwell on it any more today.

Devon shook his head and shrugged. "Nothing. I have no idea what to suggest. It is what it is, you know?" His eyes drifted out of focus for a second as he remembered. "I hate to admit it, but a part of me was thrilled. That he could do that," he explained when Rae gave him a questioning look. "It's a powerful weapon, and we're going to need all the help we can get."

Right again.

"Except, I don't want to talk about Gabriel." He smiled suddenly, leaning forward and catching her by surprise with a quick kiss. "There's actually something I've been meaning to tell you."

"Me first!" she blurted, realizing all at once that this was one of the first times they'd been alone, and there was something she'd been dying to say. "Carter proposed to my mom!"

Devon blinked. Whatever he'd been expecting, it certainly wasn't that.

"Carter, as in...*Carter*?"

"Yes." Her eyes narrowed. "You know, for the Privy Council's former golden boy, you seem to be lacking in certain key areas."

"I just can't believe it," he mused, eyes wide. Those eyes were quick to find her. "How do you feel about it? I mean... to have Carter as a stepfather? That's..."

Actually, Rae didn't know how a guy like Devon would finish that sentence.

Neglected, ignored, and pushed to the brink by his own father? Only to be temporarily disowned altogether for the simple act of falling in love?

To someone like Devon, Carter must have seemed like the perfect alternative.

Engaging, trustworthy, honorable. A man who could play the game but have genuine affection for the players as well? It was the dream.

Wasn't it?

"I don't know," she said carefully. "I mean...I guess I just thought it would never happen. They've always known each other from afar; I assumed it would always stay that way."

Devon nodded understandably, watching with concern as she bit her lip and stared worriedly out the window.

"And you know my history with Carter. We've butted heads more times than I can count. I've basically made a career of disobeying him. He's made a career of trying to put me in my place."

"But he also cares about you," Devon reminded her gently. "He may show it in a weird way, but he cares about you more than I've seen him care about anyone. Except your mom."

She smacked at his shoulder as he pulled away with a mischievous grin.

"You just had to add that last part in there, didn't you?"

"What can I say?" His eyes danced as he stayed carefully out of reach. "Who am I to stand in the way of true love? Mr. and Mrs. Andrew Carter. It has a nice ring to it."

"I'm about two seconds away from showing you what a real fireball looks like."

"Not the infamous Rae Kerrigan! I wouldn't stand a chance." He held up his hands with an adorable look of surrender, and her heart melted in spite of her wrath.

"Fine," she sniffed. "I've decided to spare you. Now, what did you want to tell me?"

She had a pretty good idea about what it was, but it was best to play it cool. She didn't want to appear over-eager, or like she was expecting anything...

"Carter asked me to go away with him for a few days."

Rae blinked and then stopped dead in her tracks.

Seemed like they were both full of surprises today.

"After the showdown at Guilder, he wants to try to collect as many ex-Presidents of the Council as possible to rally to our side. Not only would they be invaluable allies as far as tatùs go, but it would send a loud message to anyone still at Guilder who is considering joining our cause."

He looked at her expectantly, and she hurried to pull herself together. She couldn't really blame him—not when things were so up in the air, not with so much at stake. They all had a hell of a lot on their minds. But hadn't he wanted to ask her out again? Or whatever ex-couples did to get back together officially?

"Yeah, uh," she tucked her hair behind her ears, "that makes a lot of sense. When are you guys going to leave?" She could have predicted the answer even before he said it.

"Tonight. I just wanted to give you a head's up." Even as he said it he got to his feet, grabbing his jacket off the chair and slipping it over his muscular shoulders.

Rae watched the whole thing, still frozen in position on the bed. "Right, right. Well...thanks, I guess. For the head's up."

He glanced back curiously at her tone, studying her face. "What's wrong?"

"Nothing," she covered quickly. "I'm just...going to miss you. That's all."

He smiled and leaned in for a kiss. "I'm going to miss you, too. That's why I made Carter promise it's only going to be a few days."

Their lips parted as quickly as they'd come together.

"Right, well... be safe," she said glumly as he pulled open the door.

He looked back with a wry grin, the adorable dimple appearing. "Hey, look at it this way. Every second that Carter's with me is one second where he won't be here—marrying your mom."

She groaned and chucked a pillow at the door. "Never mind. I'm actually quite eager to see you go."

He chuckled and gave her a parting wave.

She waved back, feeling as though her stomach had fallen out and was rattling around somewhere on the floor.

The second the door closed behind him, she crumbled.

*Was he serious? He'd actually forgotten? And mom's not going to be here either. She's going to Scotland to start scouting out agents for the same reason...*

She lay on her back and stared up at the ceiling, counting the tiny cracks as the sun sank lower and lower in the sky. Her post-graduation life plan wasn't going at all how she and Molly had originally planned out.

No apartment. No Privy Council. No life in London. Shaky relationship. Mom set to remarry. Allied with the Knights... The list just went on and on.

She was still lying there hours later, feeling very sorry for herself, when there was a knock on the door. Half-hoping it was Devon coming back to say the whole thing was a joke, she leapt to her feet, grimacing at the pain in her stomach, and ripped the door open.

"Oh..." her face fell as she internally deflated, "...it's you."

Gabriel chuckled and shoved his way inside. "And a big hello to you, too."

"Sorry," she apologized, shutting the door behind him. "It's not that. I was just expecting someone else."

"Drake?" he teased cheerfully. "Because I don't think he's going to be up for a rematch anytime soon."

Her face tightened up in rage. "Are you kidding me? You're actually going to joke about that? Because no part of it is funny, Gabriel. You could have really—"

"I didn't come here to make jokes about it," he interrupted carelessly. "I actually came here for another reason entirely, but I knew you were angry about it, so I wanted to bring it up and get it out of the way first."

She hesitated, thrown a little off-track. His bluntness could be so derailing. "So you're here to apologize?"

"Not even remotely," he smiled charmingly, adjusting his bandage as he gazed up at her from the bed. Despite the bruises and the blood-stained gauze, there was still something overtly sexual about the way he was reclining, and she forced herself to turn away.

"We said we weren't going to antagonize them," she chided. "Before we went out to watch them train, I told everyone to keep their distance. No matter what was said."

"I know you did. I disagreed."

She gawked at him. "So you just went ahead and did whatever you wanted to do?"

Much to her surprise, he laughed softly as he pulled himself to his feet. With surprising grace, considering the fact that he'd recently been shot, he crossed the room and took her hand. "Yeah, Rae. I did. *Because*—and I can't see how the hell this would come as much of a shock—*I don't take orders from you.*"

She opened her mouth to argue, but for once came up infuriatingly blank.

He laughed again. "Little Miss Leader's got nothing to say? No, Rae. I might go along with you when I think you're right, but I certainly didn't vote you in charge. Neither did Devon, by the way," he added suddenly, with a bit too much interest. "I imagine that was a subject of much conversation after you left him behind before the Guilder fight."

She flushed defensively, and his eyes widened in delight.

"Or have you two not even talked about it yet?"

Her blood rose to a boil, and she tugged her wrist free. "Look, Alden, I really don't see how that's any of your business—"

"You haven't! That's bloody hilarious!" He clapped his hands together, grinning. "The two of you are back together, but with this huge elephant in the middle of the room. Shall we place bets on how long this is going to last? I'll give you ten to one—"

An electric shock knocked him back a step.

"Okay, five to one."

"*Gabriel*—"

"Relax, Kerrigan. I didn't come here to fight."

"Really?" Her eyes narrowed and she jutted up her chin. "Then why did you come here?"

"To take you out."

Her automatic defiance gave way to surprise. "To take me out? Where? Are we even supposed to leave the compound? And how the hell do you even have a car?"

He grinned again, eyes dancing as he took her wrist and pulled her to the door. "Details, Rae, details. We won't let ourselves be weighed down by such things."

"Hang on." She tugged them both to a stop. "Why are we going out anyway? What's the occasion?"

He looked at her in surprise, a radiant smile lighting up his face.

"It's your birthday, of course."

# Chapter 8

A mere week ago, it was likely there was virtually no one on the planet that either Rae or Gabriel couldn't best. Not a single task they couldn't achieve. Between his natural gifts and the fact that Rae had been vested with enough supernatural powers to move the sun, there was a limitless horizon in terms of things they could and couldn't do.

Today...it was an entirely different story.

"What do you mean, you can't get out the window?" Rae hissed between her teeth. "This was your freaking idea!"

The sun had fallen and she was standing in the outer courtyard, casting nervous looks around and blinking invisible whenever someone happened to walk by. Gabriel was still inside the ICU—staring up at the high window with a look of helpless determination. Despite its impossible angle, he could have leapt through it in his sleep...had he not recently had open heart surgery.

"I'm sorry," he growled back, trying to judge the best way to go about it, "not all of us can simply levitate out like you. Or have a choice of abilities—even when some of us are hybrids. I did just get *shot*, you remember."

"*You think levitation's easy?*" Rae fired back, disappearing into thin air as a patrol rounded the farthest corner on its way to the arsenal. She sent him a mental message so the guard wouldn't hear her. "You should try it sometime. There are a lot of components involved."

"I'll bet," Gabriel murmured, but she got the feeling he wasn't really listening.

"First you have to visualize the different planes around you. Then you have to somehow solidify them in your mind's eye just to take a step—"

"No, this isn't going to work."

There was a sound like a dying whale as a hole opened in the side of the wall—a hole just big enough for Gabriel to walk through to freedom. It closed the second he was through, and he looked down at her with a cheerful smirk.

"I'm sorry. You were saying something about the difficulty of levitation?"

She rolled her eyes and grabbed his hand, melting them both out of sight as the same patrol doubled back to see what all the noise was about. "Show-off..."

He squeezed her fingers, and together the two of them set off across the lawn.

Rae didn't think she'd ever get used to it—the surreal reality of simply *not* being seen. Her hair swept backwards from the wind of the people rushing past, and yet no one offered either her or Gabriel a second look.

He seemed just as delighted as she was. In fact, perhaps a bit too pleased. Rae didn't like the way he was eyeing some of the guards. Before he could trip one of them or start re-enacting scenes from Casper, the not-so-friendly ghost, she steered him sharply towards the gate of the compound.

"What now?" she whispered close to his ear, in case any of the Knights were gifted with super-human hearing. "I'm assuming you have some sort of plan to get us out of here?"

"Now is probably when we should kiss," he said practically. She shot him an impressive look of malice, but he merely shrugged. "Two star-crossed lovers, having just found their way to freedom... I'm just saying, if this was some kind of movie or book, now would be the point where we typically—"

"Gabriel, I'm giving you three seconds, and then I'm heading back to my quarters. *Alone.* You can try to explain to the guards what you're doing out here once your precious shield of invisibility is gone." She shivered in the cool night air, muttering, "I don't want to get lynched by a mob of Knights on my birthday."

He grinned. "And I promise you won't. Of course I have a plan. And it's waiting for us right on the other side of the gate."

Much quieter this time, he melted a passageway into the thick iron—creating what looked suspiciously like a heart-shaped gap for them to walk through. She gave him another withering stare before glancing back at the Knights and hurrying on through. They'd made it this far with nothing but a few latent abilities and a heap of good luck. She wasn't going to tempt fate by sticking around and demanding platonic geometrics.

"Cute," she said sarcastically, watching as he stroked the metal back into place.

Even more than most people in their early twenties, Gabriel's gift was surprisingly well-developed. If his impromptu escape antics weren't proof enough, there was always that nasty little trick he did with the iron in Drake's blood. Rae had only used his tatù a couple of times herself, but already she was struck with the innate complexity to it. It would take years of training to get even close to where he was at. And that was certainly saying something, coming from her.

He glanced back and caught her watching. "Impressed?"

"Only that no one took the time to strangle you as a child." She looked around impatiently, just waiting for a warning shot from the watchtower or a police spotlight from the sky. "Come on, seriously. What are we doing? There's nothing out here, Gabriel."

Finished with the gate, he wiped his hands on his jeans and began leading her farther down the gravel drive. "Oh ye of little faith." His eyes scanned the shrubbery by the side of the road until he apparently found what he was looking for. "If you just give it a minute, all will be revealed. And for the record,

Cromfield did try to strangle me a few times. Never succeeded, though." He waved his hand dismissively as if it was normal growing- up talk.

He came to a stop beside a mass of tangled ivy and turned back to her proudly.

Rae thought about his comment and chose to push it aside, knowing he wasn't looking for sympathy. She glanced for a moment between the twisted vines and his face. "Thanks, Gabriel..." she snapped off a leaf with a sickly smile, "it's what I've always wanted."

He rolled his eyes and chuckled. "Honestly, and you think *you* should be the leader of the group." Without another word, he swept the plants aside, revealing a sparkling sports car half-hidden in their wake.

Rae's jaw dropped open as she recognized the vehicle. Although she knew the thing was too precious for Gabriel to ever leave behind, she had no earthly idea how he'd managed to get it to the compound when he was holed up in the ICU. Much less have submerged it in vines.

"How did you..." She stopped at the look on his face. "You know what? I'm not even going to ask."

"That's the spirit!" He grinned, shutting the door behind her as she slipped into the passenger's seat. "Onwards and upwards!"

As he climbed in beside her and revved the engine, she chewed nervously on her lip. "Be honest with me, is that the morphine talking? You know, in your present condition you should probably let me drive—" Her voice choked out as she slammed backwards in her seat, gripping her armrests for dear life. Yes, the thrill of escape had firmly taken hold. But no matter how hard she tried to stay calm and be the rational one—there was something about feeling her hair streaming out behind her in the open night air that brought a giggle of excitement to her lips.

The top rolled down to match the windows, and with Gabriel laughing carelessly behind the wheel, the car practically flew out of the gnarled undergrowth and shot off down the road.

Back towards London.


"So this whole thing is for my birthday, right?"

The glittering lights of the city were just coming into view as the clock ticked ever closer to midnight, marking the official date and time of her birth. She and Gabriel hadn't spoken much on the drive, other than arguing about what music to play on the radio. They'd spent most of it basking in their newfound liberation. Rae hadn't fully realized it before, but Devon was right. The Abbey might be as nice a cage as they come, but it was still a cage. She hadn't even realized how trapped she'd felt until she was leaving it in the dust behind her.

Gabriel turned down the music—a symphonic mess of screaming and electric guitars—and glanced over at her for the first time in almost an hour. His eyes rested briefly on her flushed skin and flowing curls before his lips turned up in a small smile. "Yeah, it's for your birthday."

Rae took a moment to process this. How strange it was, locked in a compound with her closest friends and the only family she had. All that but still, the only person who'd decided to, in any way, commemorate the occasion, was Gabriel.

And yet...it begged the question.

"How did you even—"

"For fifteen years, it was my job to know absolutely everything about you. You think I couldn't figure out the day you were born? That your dad never mentioned it? Or disappeared on the day when we were younger? Your family hid the date because of a mismarked birth certificate, but we knew."

Sometimes it felt like he could read her mind. It was a trait that he and Devon shared, actually. Not that she'd ever tell either one of them that.

"But I lied to everyone," she countered, feeling a bit protective of her efforts. "Didn't tell anyone at Guilder." He remembered her father? She was dying to ask what he remembered, but held back.

"Yeah, you did." He chuckled. "First thing you do at Guilder is tell everyone, including the headmaster, this massive lie. When I found out...that was the first time I actually felt a little bit bad about wanting to kill you."

Rae blinked.

*A little more damaged than the rest of us.*

Yeah, that was an understatement.

"Fifteen years, huh?" she changed the subject, staring out the window as the car raced around another curve. "So what else do you know?"

"I know that after three cups of coffee, your fingers start shaking like a little bird."

Her head jerked around in surprise, only to see him grinning at the road. His blond hair whipped around him, shining silver in the moonlight as it danced over his emerald eyes.

She turned deliberately away, raising her voice defensively. "I'll have you know that a lot of people have that reaction to too much caffeine. It's nothing to be ashamed of—"

"I know you only pretend to like scary movies because Molly does, and you don't want her to have to watch them alone."

Rae's mask of indignation softened and she found herself smiling. "What else?"

"Let's see..." He leaned back in his seat, steering casually with one hand. "I know that you avoid using Julian's ink because it intimidates you, and you're too proud to ask for help. I know that you despise any and all types of pie. I know that you'd probably give anything in the world for that fairy on your lower back to be just a regular tattoo."

Her face flushed and she dropped her eyes to her lap.

It was a pipe dream. An errant thought she'd found herself slipping into from time to time. At first she'd felt guilty—ungrateful, even. But after everything that had happened to her and everything still to come, she couldn't help but consider the possibility.

What if she didn't have the fairy? How would her life be different? Was there a chance it would maybe be...better?

But of course, it wasn't like that was anything she could share.

She shook her head quickly, ready to rebuff and deny. "That's not true. I would never wish that—"

"I know you like this spot."

He veered suddenly off the road, parking in a clump of tall grass. Still reeling from their conversation, Rae looked around in alarm.

They were perched on a small bluff overlooking the city. It was close enough that you could hear the horns of the boats as they drifted across the river, but far enough away that the buildings themselves were just a blur of multi-colored lights.

When she'd first gotten to Guilder—first started developing feelings for Devon, and first received her tatù—she used to come up here all the time. She could sit for hours, just watching the sun make a slow orbit over the city. Thinking about her life then, dreaming about things to come.

But again...how did Gabriel know that?

She rotated slowly around to ask, but before she could a fit of giggles burst through her lips.

He was wearing an oddly lopsided hat, and was offering her another. It looked like the thing had once belonged at a construction site, but he'd used his ability to try to fashion the top into a point. While his festive intentions were apparent, the hat itself was clearly not up to the task. He'd taken a thick black marker and scribbled out, 'To be worn at all times for safety' and substituted it with, 'PARTY!' As if that wasn't enough, in his lap lay a small Tupperware container filled with what looked like chocolate cake.

"Surprise." He said it gently, almost a little shy. When she said nothing in response, he plopped the hat onto her head and pried open the Tupperware, extracting two forks from the glove box. "Yeah, it's stupid," he said before she could render a verdict. "But under the circumstances, it was the best I could do."

She took the fork he pressed into her hand, watching him avoid eye-contact while simultaneously trying to collect her thoughts.

"It's not stupid, it's...it's perfect."

More perfect than he knew.

"Thank you, Gabriel."

The faintest blush lightened the tops of his cheeks but he kept his face casual, almost to the point of indifference as he held out the container.

"It's no big deal," he said brusquely. Then, a little softer, "But I'm glad you like it."

She scooped up a forkful of cake with a huge smile, but hesitated before raising it to her lips. "You didn't try to bake this yourself, did you?"

"Oh, hell no. I conned it out of the Knights' kitchen staff."

They laughed loudly and settled themselves down on the hood of the car, gazing up at the stars and filling themselves up with chocolate as the clock slipped silently over to midnight.

In a lot of ways, it was one of the better birthdays Rae had ever had. For once she wasn't hiding it, watching in terror as a tatù she had never seen before permanently stained her skin. She wasn't stuck at Guilder, training like mad and battling enemies both outside and within. She wasn't sitting alone in her dorm, worrying like mad that her secret boyfriend had been sent out on yet another dangerous mission on the other side of the world.

This was just...peaceful. The way it was supposed to be.

"Hey," Gabriel demanded as she reached for the final bite, "share, please."

"It's my birthday," she giggled as her fork battled his to claim it.

He surrendered not an inch of ground. "Yeah, but I'm the one who got shot for you. And still managed to get cake."

"Really? You want to play this game?" She dropped her fork and sat up with a taunting smile, putting her hands on her hips. "I got stabbed, got targeted by a lunatic, got coerced into being the symbol for a hopeless war, and it's *still* my birthday! Give it up!"

He stared at her appraisingly a moment before he shoved the cake at her with a reluctant smile. "Fine, I hate chocolate anyway."

"No, you don't."

"Shut up and eat your cake, princess."

She speared it greedily with her fork—preparing to make a grand show of savoring every last morsel. But before she lifted it halfway into the air, he snatched it off with his fingers and shoved it messily into her mouth.

"Hey!" she choked, wiping bits of frosting off her face.

"I hope it was everything you wanted."

"Gabriel Alden!" She flung pieces of it his way as she tried to wipe herself clean. "I can't believe you would freakin' do that to me, today of all days—"

"You missed a spot."

His eyes twinkled and she found herself smiling in spite of her best efforts not to.

"You're a bastard."

"Happy birthday, darling."

"It's no wonder you have no friends."

"You're my friend."

"I used to be," she wiped her face on her sleeve. "Not anymore."

He chuckled and gingerly pulled himself up. "Here. You're only making it worse."

"Don't touch me," she countered, slapping his hand. "You've done quite enough."

"Rae, I say this as a friend: you've somehow managed to spread it up to your ear."

"Shut up!" she giggled as he dabbed at her face with a napkin. "No, I didn't—"

"These are the people who are supposed to help us save the world?"

Rae and Gabriel almost fell off the hood of the car as they whirled around in alarm. It was a testament to how far they'd fallen off their game that neither one of them had heard anyone coming in the midst of the cake debacle.

As it stood, there was a small group of teenagers standing in front of them, their faces half hidden in shadow. At first, Rae thought it had to be the Knights—sent out to recover them from their midnight exploits, but the group in front of her looked too young. There was something familiar about them, like she'd seen them in passing before.

Her eyes grew wide as she made the connection.

If she didn't know better, she could have sworn they were—

"Long time no see, Rae!"

The crowd parted as a tiny girl made her way down through the middle, two braids swishing on either side of her beaming smile.

"Ellie?" Rae asked in astonishment. "How the hell did you make it out of Guilder?"

Ellie put her hands on her hips, clearly concerned with a more important question. "Why are the two of you wearing those stupid hats?"

# Chapter 9

"It's even worse than you could imagine." Ellie sat on the hood now with Rae and Gabriel. The hats lay forgotten in the front seat.

The rest of the students she had brought with her—somewhere between fifteen and twenty of them—stood in a loose circle around the car. Some of them were staring at the Council's legendary fugitives, some of them were trying very hard not to.

"After you came the first time to break into Mallins' office, the whole place was on high alert," Ellie explained. "But when you guys came back with the Knights, we went into complete and total lockdown. I'm talking about agents walking students to classes. No off-campus visitations. A curfew of seven-thirty. They even shut down the library."

"They shut down the library," Rae repeated incredulously, trying to imagine the prison state the young hybrid was describing. "Why?"

Ellie exchanged a quick glance with some of the students closer to her. "Because they didn't want any of us to meet in secret and talk about what we wanted to do. They didn't want *this*."

Rae followed her eyes around the little group. They were nervous, that much was clear. Terrified, was more like it, shifting restlessly from foot to foot as they huddled in a tight mass. Half were keeping tabs on the conversation at the car, while the other half seemed to be watching the road, afraid they might have been followed.

A concern that Gabriel seemed to share.

"How did you know where we were going to be?" he asked sharply. He didn't know Ellie, and although he might be dedicated to Rae's cause, he had no loyalties to Guilder. "I only just decided it myself."

It was a fair question. Was there a chance the Council had put the Abbey under surveillance?

"We have a tracker," Ellie said quickly, gesturing a boy to her side.

He was as tall as he was gangly, an awkward combination of adolescence with a splash of freckles thrown in for good measure. He half-wilted when he saw both Rae and Gabriel staring down at him, but even so, he raised his hand in a self-conscious little wave.

"Uh, hi. I'm Jake. Ellie's boyfriend. I'm the one who found you."

*What?!*

Rae and Gabriel spoke at the same time—Gabriel to the boy, and Rae to Ellie.

"How exactly does that work?"

"You have a boyfriend?!"

Gabriel glanced at her sharply, and she leaned back. "You're right, not important." But the second he turned away, she threw Ellie a conspiratorial wink.

"How does that work?" he repeated, fixing the boy with an almost stern gaze. "Is there a chance that anyone else knows you're here?"

Jake-the-boyfriend shook his head so fast it looked like it might spin right off and roll down the hill. "Not at all. It's my ink." He extended his arm and showed them the tiny design on his arm. It was one Rae had never seen before. A tiny globe with a million glittering dots. "All I have to do is think about a person, and I know where they are."

"We couldn't find you before, even though we were trying for days," Ellie took over. "I'm guessing that wherever you're staying with the Knights, they have the place cloaked in the same kind of force-field as Guilder. But the second you left tonight, you popped up on Jake's radar." She gave him a proud grin, and Rae couldn't help but smile.

However, the fact that the students had found them was the least of their problems. It was what to do with them now that they were here.

"So I'm guessing you guys snuck out?" she asked sternly, fixing her eyes on Ellie. "That's hardly responsible, wouldn't you say?"

These were dangerous times. Kids shouldn't just be wandering around the streets.

Ellie raised her eyebrows. "And what exactly was it you two were doing tonight? You expect us to believe the Knights just let you two come and go as you please?"

Gabriel maintained a straight face, while Rae blushed and thought guiltily of the two misshaped hats sitting in the car.

"We were here on Knights business," he said without inflection.

"*Important* Knights business," Rae added, causing him to roll his eyes and Ellie to smile.

"Sure," the girl grinned, eyeing the remains of the chocolate cake.

Sometimes Rae forgot her young protégé was specifically gifted in such a way that it was impossible to pull things over on her. Wisdom and understanding. A regular bullshit detector, and the closest thing to Kyo that the Council had on its team.

Unless...Ellie wasn't on their team anymore.

"So why did you sneak out to find us?" she asked quietly, searching Ellie's eyes. "What are you kids doing here?"

Ellie glanced behind her, and for the first time since their arrival the entire group seemed to stop moving at once. Their restless energy was momentarily suspended, and all eyes travelled as one to the car—resting on Rae like she was their only hope.

"We came here to join you," Ellie said bravely, pulling herself up to her full height. "We came here to help you fight."

"She said there were about a twenty students total, and that doesn't even count faculty and the agency staff. Of those, she guesses about half would join us. And of course, that still leaves the agents themselves. Those are the people we really want to get on our side."

Rae and Gabriel were standing in the hallway outside Fodder's chamber. They had gone automatically to wake Carter first, but the second they started their story, he spun them straight around and escorted them right to the commander.

If Fodder had thought it at all odd to open his door and see two chocolate-covered teenagers and the former President of the Privy Council outside his room at three in the morning, he certainly didn't let on. Or perhaps he did, but Rae was just too excited to notice.

"That means that over half the entire population at Guilder was convinced by our story and is ready to come over. If we can just get a message to the Council, telling them when and where to meet, there's a chance we can—"

"Miss Kerrigan."

Rae recognized that tone of strained patience. It was the same one Carter used almost every time he said her name. Perhaps they taught it in some tatù leadership conference. Restraint 101.

"Yes...sir?"

Probably best to tag on the formalities at this point. The man was in his pajamas, after all.

He stifled a small sigh before sharing a glance with Carter. "Do you think perhaps it's best that we talk about a revolutionary uprising at Guilder *not* in a public hallway?"

Rae's eyes widened slightly as she glanced up and down the corridor. There was a certain degree of logic to that...

"Uh, yes. Sorry. I just...we wanted to tell you as soon as possible." She glanced back at Carter for a moment before lowering her voice. "You know, back at Guilder Carter had sort of an open-door policy. Available to us at all hours, day or night—"

"No, I most certainly did not, Miss Kerrigan," Carter replied shortly.

There it was. That tone again.

"A point I tried repeatedly to make to you and your friends, although clearly the message never sank in."

Gabriel lowered his voice respectfully. "*I* never disturbed you after hours, sir."

"No," Carter's eyes narrowed, "you simply passed on every word I told you to my mortal enemy, you filthy little spy. But you did it within office hours, so, for that, I suppose I ought to be grateful."

Rae stifled a grin as Gabriel dropped his eyes back to the carpet. Despite his repeated attempts to get back on Carter's good side, the president had never quite warmed up to him after discovering his original mission as Cromfield's spy. Gabriel had once even gone so far as to send a box of cigars...which Carter then returned, along with Gabriel's official termination of employment.

Fodder's eyes danced amusedly as they travelled from person to person, coming to rest on Rae. "Why don't we discuss this in private?"

She walked tentatively inside as he pushed open the door, her eyes quickly taking in the sparse walls and perfectly ordered belongings. Rather predictable, given what she knew about the commander. Even his books were shelved in alphabetical order by the author's last name.

The only thing that did surprise her was that the room itself was the same size as hers. No bigger, no smaller. It seemed they were called the Knights for a reason. Everyone here was on equal footing. It was something she was fast coming to respect.

"So you met with other students from Guilder," Fodder surmised, sitting down at a small desk pushed into the corner and offering Carter the other chair. Rae and Gabriel stood awkwardly on the sides. "This happened just tonight?"

"Yes," Rae said a bit reluctantly. An unfortunate part of recounting this story was that she and Gabriel would also have to confess to their crime.

But just thinking the word caused her blood to boil.

*Crime*?! It wasn't a crime. It shouldn't be a crime. They'd never asked to come here; they were taken whilst unconscious. And unless the Knights made it clear they were to be prisoners, they should be free to come and go as they wished.

Gabriel sensed her distress and quickly moved on. "We met them a little way outside the city. They came alone, and were very clear about their intent to join us."

"The thing is," Rae took over, "they're at a bit of a loss as to how to do it. You see, Mallins is running the place under something close to martial law, and even though they're not technically prisoners...it feels an awful lot like they're *not allowed to leave*."

Fodder lifted his eyes to meet hers, showing not an ounce of fear. "Feel free to speak your mind, Miss Kerrigan. We can be candid here."

She held his gaze. "I believe I just did."

"You're asking if you and your friends are something akin to political hostages," he summarized quietly. "You're asking if I am preventing you from leaving the compound."

Rae pulled in a sharp breath, but kept her voice steady. "It occurred to Gabriel and me tonight, that if we wanted to go to the city we would have to do so secretly. That if we tried to leave in the open we would be stopped, and tensions here would aggravate even further. I don't know why we would have felt that if there weren't—"

"Yes."

She froze in place, staring at Fodder in a whole new light. "Yes?" she repeated incredulously, sure that she had heard wrong.

"Yes, I've put measures in place to stop you and your friends from leaving," Fodder answered with his signature quiet calm. "It seemed the wisest course of action, considering the players on the board. The danger we're all in."

Rae's stomach dropped to the floor. "And you think some of the danger you and your people are in...is from me?"

Instead of backing down, Fodder considered her appraisingly. "When you first arrived here, yes, those were my thoughts exactly. Given your history and the information we'd gathered about you over the years, the conclusion seemed sound. Between that and the fact that when we found you—a group of five teenagers—you had already taken down over half our rival agency, I must admit I was relieved that for at least the first few hours you were with us, the five of you were under heavy sedation. Then, of course, there were other reasons—other rationalizations for keeping you here. Your injuries, for one. Your age, for another. The fact that the Council was sure to be hunting you down. All that, combined with the fact that my son..." He paused. "Point being, there were many reasons, some legitimate, some less so, for me to keep you here."

Rae felt like she was barely breathing. She had no idea why he was telling her this, and she had no idea how she should be reacting. Was now the time to run? He'd just admitted that the iron gate 'meant for their protection' was actually a cage. Shouldn't now be the time to break it?

But Carter wasn't moving. In fact, Carter looked as calm as Fodder did. A sight that filled her with a strange sort of assurance.

"So what changed?" she demanded. "Or has nothing changed at all?"

The atmosphere in the little room seemed super-charged. Like at any second, the whole thing could shatter into a million pieces. That's why both Rae and Gabriel could not have been more startled when Fodder threw back his head and chuckled.

"Say what you want about my people, Andrew," he turned to Carter, "but at least they know when it's alright to let their guard down. This is like some sort of psychological case study..."

Carter flashed Rae, and even Gabriel, an indulgent smile. "Caution is a virtue."

"That's what you call this?" Fodder parried, still grinning. "Caution?"

"I call it doing whatever it takes to stay alive."

Rae's eyes darted back and forth between both of them like a tennis match, growing increasingly anxious, until she was unable to take it anymore.

"Well that's a lovely little diagnosis you've both come up with, but I still don't see what—"

"*Everything* changed," Fodder interrupted her gently. "From the moment you spoke to me the first time. The moment I saw with my own eyes, that all the 'dangerous Kerrigan' propaganda was exactly that—propaganda. The moment we came together and formulated a plan; one to defeat Cromfield and protect every man, woman, and child gifted with a tatù. The *same* plan." He leaned back in his chair, surveying her with something bordering on affection. "We want the same things, Miss Kerrigan. When I realized that, everything changed."

Rae stared back at him in silence, completely taken aback by both his sincerity and his frank conclusions about the future, and where they all stood. This was the man to have on their side, she thought suddenly. This—coming here—was perhaps the only fortunate turn of events she and her friends had stumbled across in a long time.

"There are still guards outside our doors." Gabriel was less convinced, and with his history she hardly blamed him. Devon was right. Both he and Angel needed more time to reconcile with these sorts of things. They probably always would. "A patrol passes by the gate every seventeen minutes on the dot. Passes by the *interior* of the gate. They're keeping people in, not out." His eyes flashed as he stared Fodder down. "What do you have to say about that?"

"*That*," Carter pushed slowly to his feet, "was my idea."

"Your idea?" Rae couldn't believe it. "Why would you do something like that?"

He gave her a calculating stare, and all at once she felt like she was just a student again. Just a student talking to her headmaster. It was comforting and chilling, all at the same time.

"I suggested it," he explained, "because, unlike Commander Fodder here, I happen to know you. I was completely unsurprised when you showed up at my door this evening, and I'll be completely unsurprised should it happen again. That will not stop me, however, from doing everything in my power to prevent you children from leaving."

Gabriel shook his head slowly. "But why—"

"Because you are being hunted by the Council."

A profound silence followed this remark.

"Since the day you started at Guider, Rae, you've been in danger. Gabriel, from what I know of your past, I would expect you've been in danger for longer than that. You've spent years of your lives out-smarting and out-maneuvering foe after foe—both on official Council business, and within your own lives. You no stranger to this, I understand that. But what you have to understand is this: the Council isn't like anything that's ever hunted you before. The resources, the man-power, the personal knowledge of you and your friends. A friend turned enemy is the most dangerous sort."

Gabriel still looked hesitant, but Rae was beginning to understand. "So you lock the gate..."

"...because I don't want to see any of you get hurt again." Carter's voice was soft and filled with an emotion that he usually kept at bay. "I would lock you all in your rooms if I could."

That essentially ended the meeting. As they were getting up to go, Fodder promised that he would talk over Guider extraction plans for the people who wanted to defect with his counselors and they'd discuss it the next few days. Other than that, they were all officially free to come and go as they pleased...the Knights' ban had lifted. Though Carter would have seen it otherwise.

They bid the commander goodnight and set off quickly down the hall—Rae, Gabriel, and Carter—heading back to their own rooms. They didn't speak, but as they passed the ICU and Gabriel turned to go, Carter caught him suddenly by the shoulder.

He turned around in surprise, half-bracing himself for a reprimand, but Carter had just three simple words to say to him.

"Even you, Gabriel."

Gabriel's lips parted, but for one of the first times Rae could remember he could think of nothing to say. He was still staring in shock as the door swung shut between them.

"Well..." Rae began as the two of them continued down the hall, "that was unexpected."

Carter shot her a look. "My words to Gabriel, or your most recent outburst in front of the Commander of the Xavier Knights?"

"Outburst?!" she cried. "The man admitted to keeping us prisoner. I was simply asking why—"

"—in your customary, inflammatory way."

*Customary, inflammatory way? Okay, true. But it's not like I'm ever going to admit to it.*

"Seems like you're going to have to get used to that," Rae said softly. "If you're going to be in the family and all..."

Carter looked like he'd swallowed a bug. "Beth told you," he finally managed to choke, pulling her gently to a stop.

Rae's eyebrows lifted in surprised. Seems that dear ol' Mom had forgotten a thing or two before skipping off to Scotland.

"She didn't tell you that she told me?"

"No..." Carter closed his eyes with a painful grimace. "Why would she do that?"

*Why indeed.*

Rae dug the toe of her boot nervously into the floor, unsure of what to do. Over the last few years, she and Carter had found themselves in almost every situation imaginable. But that didn't mean—by any stretch of the imagination—that they were ready for something like this.

When she looked back up, he was watching her nervously.

A look of supreme uncertainty clouded his always-certain face. "I'd wanted to tell you with your mother. In fact, I'd wanted to ask you for permission long before that," he confessed softly.

"Ask me for permission?" Rae was genuinely surprised.

"Of course!" Carter's uncertainty grew. The man had never been particularly good at showing his feelings, and situations like this were obviously a nightmare. "Rae...you know that I care about you and your mother very much. But I would never want to do anything to come between—"

"I think it's a great idea."

"Rae, you're not hearing me. I'm saying that my top priority is...I'm sorry." He stopped suddenly and backtracked. "What did you say?"

Rae fought back a smile. "You love my mother, and she loves you. You make each other incredibly happy. I think...I think it's a great idea."

"You do?" Carter almost laughed in relief. His entire face was contorted in a smile so wide Rae didn't think his mouth would ever recover. "Well, that's...wonderful news."

"As long as it means I get to know the launch codes and stuff. You know... family secrets."

There was a huge pause.

"That was a joke, sir."

"Right," he laughed nervously, "of course. You know, we'll probably have to do something about you calling me 'sir' as well."

Rae's eyes darted to the side as she tried to think what else in the world she would possibly call him. "Let's...just take things one step at a time."

"Agreed." He nodded briskly. "Well, in that case, you'd better get some sleep. I'm sure you're set to have more physical therapy in the morning."

She grinned wickedly. "You mean more *walking*? Yeah, I think I've mastered that."

He smiled as well. "Yes, well, at any rate...goodnight, Rae."

"Goodnight...Carter."

He looked like he was about to give her a hug, but in the end it was so awkward that the both of them ended up just shaking hands. It was hard to say who walked away faster, but even though neither one could see, they both walked away with huge, impossible smiles.

"You seriously have no idea how bad this timing is, Molls. Carter just told me that he doesn't want any of us leaving. It's going to look like—"

Molly braced her hands against her hips. "I don't care what it looks like, someone has to go and sign our termination agreement. Otherwise the penthouse goes into foreclosure, or the bank seizes it, or something else happens where we end up losing the whole thing altogether."

Rae chewed on her bottom lip, trapped between two people who most definitely knew how to hold a grudge. "Well, why can't *you* go?" she finally asked, succumbing to childish misdirection.

Molly smirked. "Really? The entire Council is on our tale and you're going to ask me to go to London by myself to sign the papers? Risk my life just for an apartment?"

"...you're asking me to go."

"You've risked your life for a lot less." Molly sniffed self-importantly. "And we both know this is never going to come to that. This all boils down to the fact that you don't want to disappoint dear ol' Dad."

Rae met her devilish grin with a cold stare. "That was entirely uncalled for."

"You'd better get used to it. It's only a matter of time before he moves into the house in Scotland, he and your mom adopt a puppy, one thing leads to another, and then—"

"Okay, fine—I'll go! Just...never finish that sentence." Rae conjured herself a purse and slung it across her shoulder with the expression of a martyr.

But in truth, she would have gone for a lot less. Anything to set Molly's mind at ease.

To say that Molly hadn't been herself since the fight at Guilder was an understatement of massive proportions. Not only had she deliberately stayed away from every meeting that had happened at the compound—not the least of which included the trip to Guilder—but she had refused to come to training as well. Something about...she didn't think she was physically up to it yet after the fight. Something that everyone who knew her knew was an absolute lie.

Rae had tried to talk to Luke about it, but he seemed just as baffled as her. 'People handle trauma in different ways,' he'd said. Although completely unsatisfied with this answer, Rae had let it go. The poor guy was just as lost as the rest of them. But Rae knew firsthand how much 'trauma' Molly was capable of handling and this didn't even scratch the surface. Something was just *wrong*, that's all there was to it. In fact, since they'd gotten back, she'd yet to see Molly even use her tatù.

"If anyone asks where I am, just say I'm locked in my room. Meditating or something," she continued as she pushed open the door. "With any luck, I'll be back before anyone notices."

"Thanks, Rae," Molly said quietly.

Rae turned around to see her friend staring down at the floor, lost in a sea of undetermined emotions, trying so hard to hold it all in. "Anytime," she promised. Her hand tightened on the frame as she paused. "And Molls?"

Molly looked up. "Yeah?"

"Everything..." Rae hesitated, not sure herself but wanted to make the anxiety on her friends face disappear. "This is all going to be okay. You know that, right?"

"Yeah, sure." Molly forced a smile. "Now go sign the deed so we can be officially homeless."

"That's the spirit."

In an act of most uncharacteristic charity, Gabriel actually allowed Rae to drive his car into the city. At first, he had flat-out refused, but then she'd said it was a favor to Molly. Like the rest of them, he was feeling inexplicably protective of Molly, and he'd handed over the keys without another word. The gate swung open automatically to let her out, and as she sailed past one of the guards in the watchtower gave her a solemn nod.

The entire ride there, she worked hard to compartmentalize what she was about to do. She didn't want to give up the penthouse. She happened to love the penthouse. And in the whirlwind of everything that had happened since graduation, she felt as though she hadn't really been able to give the place a real shot.

But everything that Molly was saying made sense, and especially since Molly was the one who was saying it, she parked in a loading zone and marched into the lobby with steely nerves and fresh determination. She'd just sign the papers and be done with it. In and out. Simple as that.

...there was just one little thing she'd failed to take into account.

"Oh, Miss Kerrigan!"

She looked up just in time to see Raphael, their faithful lobby attendant, barrel into her. She sucked in a tight breath as he squeezed the life out of her, sobbing openly into her shoulder.

"I cried for hours when I heard the news," he finally gasped, pulling away, "I just can't believe it. Both you and Molly—gone forever?! What am I going to do? How am I going to pass the time? Your place was like a soap-opera. It gave the whole building a little sparkle."

Rae's face broke into an unexpected smile as she gave the man another hug. In a way, it was nice to know that someone else was going to miss them here as much as she was. It gave it a certain kind of closure. "You know we'll come back and visit all the time," she promised. "Julian and Devon still live right down the street. And I don't think you've even officially met Angel yet."

"The girl with the white-blond hair?" he asked, looking started. "Honey, I don't want to. I think we both know that I'm not one to judge, but that girl seems a bit too high-strung."

Rae looked from the deep bruises beneath his eyes to the tears streaming down his cheeks.

*Angel* was a bit high-strung? The two of them could form a club.

"Well, anyway, I'm just here to sign the termination papers..."

"Oh, right."

He pulled them down from a shelf and watched sadly as she scribbled her name. When she was finished, he gave her another tight hug before walking swiftly away, overcome with the grief of it all. "Don't be a stranger, okay?" he called over his shoulder, probably heading to his locker to grab some sort of sedative. "I still want to hear all the latest news—"

The door swung shut behind him, cutting off his pleas and leaving Rae standing alone in the lobby; homeless, and suddenly feeling a little lost. A chapter in their lives was closing and it had barely started.

She wandered aimlessly outside, not quite ready to drive back to the compound yet. Although the paperwork now said otherwise, she still felt as though this place was her home, and there was a certain security just in being close. She half-considered wandering over to Devon and Julian's place—even though she knew it was locked—but walked across the street and took a seat on a park bench instead, gazing up at her old balcony. The place where she used to live.

The place where she still wanted to live.

How could it be that, suddenly, it was just gone? Was anything ever going to start to feel like home?

She sat there for a long while, gazing up at the building as a gentle autumn breeze played with her hair. The bench was on the park side of the street, and pleasantly shaded. There were dozens of people coming and going at this time of day, so when a middle-aged man came and sat down on the other side, she hardly took notice.

"Moving in?" he asked pleasantly.

She smiled politely still staring up at the lonely balcony up top. She sighed. "Moving out, actually."

"I'm sorry to hear that. This is a lovely spot."

She nodded sadly and they lapsed back into silence, each one taking in the afternoon with quiet thought.

After a few minutes, the man finally broke it. "I knew a girl once, she was about your age, and she would have given anything to have lived in a place like that."

"Oh, yeah?" Rae answered, barely listening. She glanced down and stared at the man's hands, his nails perfectly manicured.

The man chuckled. "As extravagant as it seems, she thought it would make her life seem more normal. Something she desired above all things."

A faint shiver ran across Rae's skin and she realized she'd stopped breathing. Her eyes fixed on the building as the rest of her turned to perfect stone. Listening. And waiting.

"Why did she want so badly to be normal?" the man continued, seemingly oblivious to the change. "I've asked myself that question again and again. What's so great about being *normal*? Why was it something that this extraordinary girl prized so highly? And then, like a bolt of lightning, the answer hit me. All at once. Do you want to know what it was?"

It felt as if a cold hand was holding Rae in place. Keeping her from moving. Stopping her from running. In her periphery, she saw the man turning slowly towards her, fixing her in his sights. "What was it?" she whispered, suddenly terrified to know the answer.

"Time," he said simply. "The answer was she needed time."

Like pushing together opposing magnets, Rae dragged her eyes away from her old home, twisting on the bench so she could see the man straight on.

He met her eyes with a smile.

"Time's up, Rae."

# Chapter 10

*Jonathon Cromfield.*

Rae had time for a single scream. One sound before her world came crashing down. A single cry that was drowned out in the pleasant hum of London traffic.

The scream never made it out of the park.

The syringe was in and out of her before she realized what was happening—deadening her muscles with a dull ache that seemed to radiate out from the center of her body, consuming everything in its path. She felt the same paralyzing numbness she'd come to associate with Angel's freezing ability. In fact, the feeling was so familiar that she was suddenly sure of what was coursing through her veins. *Use your tatù, Rae! Do something. Don't just sit here frozen. Fight it!*

The same paralyzing agent that Cromfield gave to all the hybrids before he took what he needed from them and left them in the dust. She couldn't move. From fear and the needle.

"Don't fight it, my dear." He stroked back her hair—appearing, for all the world to see, as a doting father, just having a pleasant talk with his daughter on a balmy London afternoon. Doting, perhaps, but cautious. No matter what happened, he was careful not to touch her skin. "I've believe it's even more unpleasant when you fight it."

She fought it anyway, but the harder she tried resist the more the freeze tightened its grasp. A dose of Angel's blood was far more powerful than the tatù itself. She tried to break free like she had the first time they'd gone after Angel. Except there was something new in this concoction. It was like working against a vacuum. One after another, her limbs went completely numb, starting with her feet and working its way up. Before she knew it, Cromfield was leaning her gently back against the bench, propping her head up so she wouldn't fall over.

*Come on, Rae. Get it together! You know it can't freeze everything! It can't freeze your mind! Or your heart.*

With a strength that surprised even her, she centered all her focus on a single tatù, drawing strength from her mother. There was what felt like an actual tearing inside her, but the next second, a wave of blue flames shot over the bench, engulfing Cromfield before her very eyes.

*Now run,* she thought in a wave of panic, eyes darting around the street to make sure no one had seen. *Screw the sedative and run, before he has a chance to heal himself. This might be your only chance—*

A slow chuckle ripped her away from the fantasy.

As if brushing off a pesky layer of dust, Cromfield slowly patted down his arms and legs, extinguishing the lethal fire. Rae looked on in horror. She knew the man couldn't die any more than she could. But her mother's ink was one of the most powerful in her collection. If that couldn't even slow him down, then...

"You forget, sweet one; I wielded Bethany Kerrigan's flames long before you did. As such, I'm equally immune to their fire."

An image of her mother, passed out in the roaring flames that extinguished Rae's childhood, flashed through her mind and a deep hatred swelled in her chest. "Don't call me that," she growled, fighting the paralysis with everything she had. "And don't you dare talk about my mother."

"Look at you!" Cromfield seemed genuinely impressed. "Rae, this is exactly what I was talking about when I said you were extraordinary. What other person in the world could manage to talk with our little Angel's blood running through their veins? It's truly a sight to behold."

A searing pain shot through Rae's jaw as she tried to speak again. "Let's see if you can manage it yourself," she hissed. "Make it an even playing field."

He laughed again, a deep, booming laugh that in any other circumstance would have been considered something close to jovial. The kind of laugh that belonged to a kindly uncle, or a favorite teacher at school. The kind of laugh that had no place in this park.

"No, sweetheart, I don't think I will. You see, I came here today with the intention only to speak to you, not to harm you in any way. I would never harm you, Rae. You have to know that. However, judging by the look on your face, I'm guessing you'd like nothing better than to see me dead." He chuckled again, as if the thought amused him greatly. "Clearly, that's not something I can allow, and I also don't want *you* getting hurt in the process of trying to hurt *me*—hence the sedative."

Rae's body was shaking now, shutting down from all the strain. "How very thoughtful of you," she managed before her voice cut out entirely.

"There, there." He caught one of her dark curls and twirled it absentmindedly between his fingers. "Just rest now. You're going to need your strength."

A pair of tears slipped down her cheeks and his face tightened with concern as he wiped them away, using his woolen sleeve to prevent any sort of contact.

"Rae," he said gently. How could a man so vicious be so gentle? "Please don't cry. There's nothing to cry about, I promise you. I know you're worried about your friends. You're worried about what will happen to them in the days to come. Just know this: I'll not harm anyone—not a single person you love—as long as they don't stand in our way. You have my word."

A horrific chill slid down her back, but she was unable to shiver. She was unable to even breathe as the monster sat there and touched her.

"That pardon applies to everyone. Molly, Carter, your mother, Julian..."

Her throat tightened a little more with every name that he said, choking off her sobs as his voice caressed them all in a way that said he knew far too much about them.

"Even my wayward children—Gabriel, Angel. Even they will be spared, if it pleases you."

The image of it flashed through Rae's mind. A final attack. Gabriel and Angel racing towards her, struck down by the very man who'd stolen away their very lives.

Cromfield leaned down, into her line of sight. "Even Devon."

Her head jerked one final time of its own accord as every inch of her ached to reach out and strangle this man with her bare hands. He didn't get to say that name. *You bastard,* she hissed mentally.

"Yes," he said quietly, smiling ironically, "even your precious Devon could be saved. In fact, I would still allow you to see him from time to time. Given that you spend the rest of that time with me." Without seeming to think about it, he reached out and nearly stroked a finger down the side of her cheek. If she leaned slightly, he would be touching her.

Her eyes snapped shut as another rush of tears fell to the ground. *Devon!* she screamed silently, wishing it would all just end. *Devon, come find me!*

"I wanted to give you a chance to have your normal life. But now..." he gazed up at her empty home, "surely you see that's not possible. So I'm not waiting any longer." He straightened up suddenly, as if someone had sounded an alarm. "The time for waiting has passed, my dear. The time for action is upon us. You and I are standing on the brink of a new world order, and, like it or not, you are a critical part of that." Without breaking eye contact, he kissed two of his fingers and leaned close, blowing them over her lips.

It felt like a caress against them and she shuddered as if he'd touched her. A heart-wrenching cry echoed in her frozen throat—a cry no one could hear.

"Stay well, my dear. You'll be hearing from me soon."

With a parting smile, he pushed to his feet and set off through the park, ambling along with his hands in his pockets, not a care in the world. But before he disappeared from sight entirely, he turned around with a final message.

"And, Rae...please keep in mind what I said about your friends. There's no reason for everyone to die."

With that, he vanished into the trees, leaving a frozen, quaking Rae in his wake.

She was going to kill him. Tear him limb from limb and rip his head off if she had to.

Over a hundred people must have walked past Rae over the course of the next hour, people who had no idea that she wasn't sitting there, that she was *frozen* on the park bench. She watched Gabriel's car get ticketed, and then towed out of the loading zone. She felt her phone buzz deep in her pocket. Molly, no doubt, wondering what was taking so long.

However, despite the urgency to get up, despite the fact that she could feel the sedative beginning to fade...a part of her didn't see the point.

From the moment she turned sixteen, she had been granted the ability to wield every single power on the planet. There was no limit to what she could do, or how much she could achieve. If she put her mind to something, there was not a single obstacle that could stand in her way.

Except one.

But just that one...changed everything.

It didn't matter how many powers she had. It didn't matter if she absorbed the tatùs of every single person alive and breathing today.

Cromfield was always going to be stronger.

For every power she had, he had ten. For every year she'd been alive to gather them, he'd been alive decades more. For every step that she planned, he was five steps ahead.

And even if she figured all that out, even if she somehow found a way to break through all the infinite impossibilities and land the final, lethal blow...it wouldn't be lethal at all.

Because the man couldn't die.

So what the hell were they doing here?

She ignored a passing wave of curious pedestrians as a flood of angry tears poured down her face. Instead, she focused on regaining control of her limbs, one inch at a time. She started with her feet, wiggling her toes as she chanted the defeatist mantra over and over in her head.

*Doesn't matter how many powers I have, it'll never be enough. Doesn't matter how many powers I have, it'll never be enough. Doesn't matter how many damn powers I freakin' have, it'll never be en—*

A sudden gasp ripped through her throat, and her body fell right off the bench. She hit the ground hard on her side, but was completely immune to the shooting pain that followed. She was on another level of thought altogether. Her mind shouting down a million useless possibilities as a single shining idea rose to the surface.

*Maybe it isn't about having a million powers. Maybe it's about having just one power.*

*The right power.*

"Excuse me, miss? Are you alright?"

With supreme effort, Rae twisted up her head to see an ancient-looking woman kneeling over her in concern. As the remainder of the sedative drained slowly from her limbs, she slowly pulled herself up, leaning on the woman's cane for temporary support. "No," she finally panted once she was standing, "but I'm going to be."

She didn't think she'd ever say it. No—she didn't think the thought would ever, *ever* cross her mind. But here it was. A cosmic twist of fate.

She needed to see Victor Mallins.


There was no time to hail down a cab. Or time to call for backup. There was no bloody time to do anything other than dart behind a tree and let her body take to the skies, lifting above the London smog on the wings of an eagle.

If she couldn't gather enough powers to beat Cromfield, then she would just have to make sure that she was immune to the powers he already had. Her scarcely-healed incision burned against her lower stomach as a dull reminder. If she was immune to his powers, then he would have to fight her hand to hand. And if they were fighting hand to hand, and he wasn't able to heal...

*And to think, if Mallins hadn't stabbed me in the stomach, I never would've gotten the idea. Turns out the little bastard was the key all along. Kind of ironic, isn't it?*

Even as she thought the words she increased her speed, racing through the clouds back towards Guilder. She couldn't believe that Cromfield hadn't already anticipated this move. He'd safeguarded against everything else except the one thing that could finally bring him to justice?

No, she didn't buy that. This was a stroke of sheer good luck, but it was ending fast. There was only a brief window of opportunity, and if she didn't get there in time...

Before it even seemed possible, she heard the sounds of the school down below. She swooped lower and lower in the sky, until she finally saw the glistening dome of the Oratory.

*Yes,* she thought with a surge of hope. *I made it.*

But the closer she got, the more she realized something was wrong. The stir of voices she'd heard before wasn't the sound of students. In fact, as she dipped below the clouds she realized she didn't see a single student on the ground. She saw agents instead.

In a blur of speed, she landed behind one of the tall oak trees and quickly conjured herself some clothes. Then she joined the flood of people darting toward the southern lawn. The whole place was in such an uproar that no one even noticed who she was—not until she'd pushed her way all the way through the crowd to see what the commotion was about.

The second she got through, she stopped cold.

Victor Mallins... dead.

Lying in a pool of his own blood.

She shrank back a few steps, staring in shock. His withered old face was cracked open at the mouth, a strange look of triumph lighting his cold features in a final farewell. Then the implications of his death hit her like a punch to the face.

If he was dead, that meant his tatù was gone forever from the world. And if immunity was no longer on the table, how was she supposed to...

"That's Rae Kerrigan!"

"Kerrigan—do you see her?!"

"FREEZE!"

"Standing next to Cromfield!"

"DON'T MOVE! DON'T EVEN THINK ABOUT MOVING!"

She lifted her head to see a hundred guns pointed directly at her face, the men behind them aiming to kill. In a mixture of surrender and exhaustion, she collapsed to her knees, raising her hands behind her head with a shrill, *"I didn't do it!"*

"READY!"

She couldn't believe it. They were going to shoot her right here on the lawn.

"AIM!"

She closed her eyes and tried to think of something else. Anything else. Anything to distract her from what was about to come. A single face floated through her mind, and she let out all the air in her chest with a gentle smile.

"WAIT!"

A different voice rang through the crowd, one she knew as well as her own. By the time she opened her eyes, the face she had been picturing was streaking towards her at the speed of light, eyes fastened on hers as it threw itself between her and guns.

"PLEASE!" Devon cried again, placing his body over hers so that every inch of her skin was covered. "PLEASE DON'T SHOOT!"

"Devon," she whispered, "it wasn't me. It was Cromfield."

His arms wrapped around her neck, pulling her even tighter into his chest. She could feel his heart pounding through his thin shirt. Despite the speed at which he'd tackled her, he was barely even breathing.

"Put down your guns!" another voice commanded, almost as familiar as the first. "Now!"

There was a soft crunch of footsteps as another person stepped in front of Devon. Then another. Then another.

By the time Rae lifted her head, every single person she loved was standing in between her and the firing squad.

Julian, Angel, Gabriel, Molly. Carter.

But then there were others there as well; others who had less reason to be.

Luke. Commander Fodder. Even Drake—standing with the rest.

A strangled sob ripped through Rae's chest and Devon gripped her tighter.

"I didn't do it," she cried again. "I swear—I didn't do it."

"No, she didn't."

There was a murmur through the crowd as another man walked through the middle, a man Rae had seen in passing a hundred times, but had never put a name to until now.

Louis Keene.

In perfect unison, the Guider guards lowered their guns.

"I saw the man who did..." There was a very peculiar look on his face, the look of someone who couldn't quite reconcile what they'd just seen. "A man I know only from our history books. I didn't think it was possible..."

Like a person venturing out onto a frozen lake, Carter lowered his hands and approached slowly, keeping himself between Rae and the gunmen all the while.

"Louis?" he asked tentatively. "You saw?"

Keene looked up in a daze, staring at Carter like he'd never seen him before. "From my office. I was just...he's really alive, isn't he? Jonathon Cromfield?"

A collective shiver ran through the PC agents, and Rae pressed her face against Devon's chest in utter exhaustion.

*They finally believed... They finally believed...*

"Yes, it was." Carter put his arm around the man's shoulders, steering him casually towards Commander Fodder to make an official introduction. "Louis, we need to talk."

And just like that, the crowd dispersed. There were no divisions to it. No partisan lines. Everyone drifted out together. The Council and the Knights alike. All at a loss from what they'd just witnessed. All dazed by the horror of it.

In a single motion, Rae was lifted to her feet. She saw Julian talking to Devon, trying to make sure that she was alright, but she couldn't hear anything. Her ears were still ringing from the shots that weren't fired. Gabriel was walking towards them through the crowd, but he stopped when he saw her standing in Devon's arms.

A second later, he disappeared.

"He just walked in here and did this."

It was the first sound to cut through the ringing. Rae looked up to see Devon still staring at Mallins, a look of complete astonishment written across his face. "He just walked in here and did this," he said again. "He's that powerful."

Rae had nothing to say in response. She merely shivered again and buried her face in his chest.

He looked down at once, arms coming up automatically to protect her. "Come on," he murmured, "let's get you home."

She looked up in a daze as he swept her off her feet and carried her over the grass.

"Where's that?"

He marched towards the horizon, a fiery look in his eyes. "It's wherever we're together."

# Chapter 11

Rae's eyes slowly blinked open and closed before finally focusing on the cracked lines in the ceiling. The same lines travelled through every room in the Abbey—a single connecting thread, banding the whole thing together. Judging by the general look of the place, the compound had to be very old—but these lines were the only signs of it. Everything else had been refurnished and repainted and restructured into a state-of-the-art military facility. You could house an army in the place. You could fend off a war. Strangely enough, Rae took comfort in the lines. If nothing else, they proved the place had lasted this long.

The crisp smell of fresh air and wet stone wafted in through the window, along with the distant sound of men and women coming together to talk and train. But the sky was a uniform 'English white,' providing no clue as to the hour, and Rae had no idea what time it was.

*Why didn't anyone wake me up,* she wondered as she sat up on the mattress and pulled a thick bathrobe over her arms. There was still an imprint in the sheets beside her where Devon had slept, but she was alone. *They probably think I'm still too fragile from what happened last night.*

It wasn't an outrageous assumption. Truth be told, Rae had very little memory of exactly what had happened after she left Guilder last night. It came back to her in fractured images, cracked though consistent, like the line in the ceiling, continuing its journey through her mind.

Devon carrying her through the crowd. Carter shouting something as they left. The fact that Guilder's entire ancient fence had been ripped right out of the ground—a fact she hadn't noticed when she'd flown in as a bird. In hindsight, that was probably the only reason she was able to get through the domed force-field that curved up over the place. Otherwise, her tatù would have been stripped and she would have fallen hundreds of feet to the ground as a human.

However, despite all the chaos that surrounded her memories, the thing that struck Rae most was the people. The looks on their faces. A hundred different faces. A hundred different ages, ethnicities, and sizes; yet, somehow, they all looked exactly the same.

Resolved.

Devon looked that way, too. The hard lines etched into the sides of his mouth made him look years older than he was. A veritable silver bullet, making his way through the crowd.

Rae shook her head and refused to think any further. That was yesterday. As of this morning, 'yesterday' was officially something she could categorize as 'the past' and make every attempt to move forward. It wouldn't help to dwell. It wouldn't help to be shocked, or scared, or any of a number of things that went along with the image side by side.

Now was the time for action. Now was the time for momentum.

Now was the time to unite.

*Which again begs the question why no one woke me up.*

"Devon?" she called tentatively as she conjured herself a black running suit and slipped it on. There was no answer, but she hadn't really expected there to be. There was something a little too resolved about Devon's face last night, and she figured she would have to sort that mess out before even starting to handle the rest.

Her man tended to take things personally. And when those things were a hundred guns aimed at her head, he tended to take them very personally.

Sweeping her hair up into an efficient ponytail, she pushed open the door and set off down the long, curving corridor.

From the second she walked across the threshold, she felt the change.

She was starting to recognize the people she saw in the halls, and they were starting to recognize her. Not as a scary 'Kerrigan' or a rogue Privy Council agent, but as Rae. The dark-haired girl with the huge bandage who lived in room 4C. Several hands lifted in a cursory greeting as she passed, and a few people even offered a tentative, "You doing okay?" The now-familiar smell of the mess hall's inedible breakfast buffet triggered up her gag reflex, and by the time she made it to the door that led to the outdoor courtyard, she was almost beginning to smile.

She might have officially lost her home yesterday, but she wouldn't write off the whole concept so quickly. This place might just be a contender. This place might just have what it takes.

*Apparently, she wasn't the only one who thought so...*

A gentle mist settled upon her the second she stepped outside, but that's not the reason she froze. She froze in her tracks because of what she saw going on at the other end of the practice field.

Angel, Julian, Gabriel, and Luke were all standing out on the grass, training with the Knights.

For a second, Rae just watched—a strange sort of pride swelling up in her chest. It's not like they were going through their regular routines; it would be quite a while before their injuries had healed enough for them to do that. But they were going through the motions—assuming more of a teaching role than a student's—taking their Abbey counterparts through each attack, step by step.

What's more...the Knights were really listening.

It had become instantly clear from the second the gang arrived at the Abbey that there were some major discrepancies in terms of how both the Knights and the Privy Council chose to get things done. There was a reason the PC was the higher-ranked agency. There was a reason they got things like the royal protection contracts and the Knights didn't. They pushed harder, demanded more, and were—Rae hated to say it—a lot more cavalier when it came to the lives of their agents, no matter how young or inexperienced they were. They quite simply demanded the best.

But after spending time with the Knights, Rae wasn't so sure they'd won the title.

Sure, she and her friends were technically better trained than the agents here at the Abbey, but what they'd acquired in skill they'd lost in other areas. Security. Trust. Freedom. These were things the Knights had in spades.

Rae had always wondered why, when the PC was the 'superior' agency, many men and women still chose to align themselves with the Knights. Now she knew.

There were no secrets here. No abilities that people had to hide. Hybrids were hybrids out in the open. Not that there were many, but people like Kyo were lauded, not despised. The families of each of the agents knew exactly what they were, and what they were doing—whether they had a tatù or not. Luke was technically an agent himself, though not marked. Devon had mentioned at one point last night that Luke actually had an older brother who was the one with the ink. There was a spirit of inclusion with the Knights that Guilder had always lacked. A feeling of long-term sustainability, a contentedness that resided in the hearts of the agents rather than in their performance record.

In a way, it's exactly what she and Devon had always talked about. Had always been hoping for. A place where they could be who they were and love who they wanted, while still serving the cause. It was a reform they'd always hoped the Council would one day adopt, but knew, deep down, would never come to pass.

"Rae!" Julian trotted over the moment he saw her, drawing the eyes of several curious agents before they resumed their training. The second he made it across the grass, he took her by the shoulder and looked her up and down. "Hey! How are you feeling?"

His arm was still in a sling and the bruises on his face had yet to heal, but there was something different about him today. His skin was flushed and his eyes were sparkling with the excitement of something Rae could only describe as 'proactive motion.' They were finally *doing* something. They had finally broken through the barrier and were moving forward as one.

She smiled and gestured down to herself, wincing only slightly when she pulled against the stitches still holding her stomach together. "You know me, never better. Ready to go."

His dark eyes met hers with a faint smile. "You forget—I *do* know you. How are you feeling?"

She hesitated, eyes sweeping the field. "Where's Devon?" she asked, dodging the question.

Julian followed her gaze, resting on Angel for a moment—who was demonstrating a lethal flying kick—before turning back to Rae. "I don't know. He didn't come out with the rest of us. I assumed he was with you."

Rae tapped her foot nervously, growing more and more anxious by the moment. She couldn't shake the look on his face the other day. The way he kept murmuring, 'he's too powerful,' almost to himself. She knew Devon was taking this personally, but she was starting to worry he was taking 'personally' to a whole other level. To a dark, internal place she couldn't follow.

"Could you check for me?" she asked. "I'm a little...could you just check?"

She didn't make Julian do this sort of thing very often. It was an invasion of privacy that he had long ago sworn to avoid whenever possible. But until she got her hands on Ellie's boyfriend's handy tracking ability, she'd still need a little help. As it stood, she had no trouble whatsoever invading someone's privacy if she thought there might be a good reason behind it.

Julian studied her face for a moment. "Sure."

Extending his good arm slightly to keep his balance, his eyes faded out to white. He began to sway in the gentle breeze and Rae automatically took his hand to keep him centered.

The first time she'd seen him do this, it had scared the shit out of her. He looked almost like a ghost. A handsome ghost, perfect in every way, except for his creepy, white eyes. Now, she was so used to it that she barely noticed the change. It was simply another part of him. Something as natural as breathing or thought.

But whatever Julian was seeing, he certainly didn't like it. His forehead creased in concentration, and even before he snapped back into the present, he was already starting to frown. "I don't know... I can't see him."

Rae dropped his hand in alarm. "What do you mean, you can't see him?"

"It's nothing like that," Julian said quickly, still a bit distracted as he tried to re-center. "He's deliberately keeping me out. Deliberately not making any pre-meditated decisions I can follow."

Rae took a step back, impressed in spite of herself. "Is that even possible?"

Julian rolled his eyes with a long-suffering sigh. "You'd be surprised. He figured out how to do it when we were stationed together your senior year. I was having trouble controlling the frequency of my visions, not seeing everything about everyone, and he was determined to keep some things private. Mainly...you."

*Yeah...I bet he wanted to keep that private.*

A little grin flashed across Rae's face as she thought about what it must have been like. Julian and Devon sitting in one of a hundred nameless hotel rooms, in one of a hundred nameless countries. Jules—trying like mad to keep his visions under control. Devon—trying like mad to figure out a way to outfox him so he could keep on secretly dating Rae.

As if Julian didn't already know.

"Anyway, it's certainly not easy, but if anyone can do it, he can." Julian's eyes flickered back to the training group, following along. He looked annoyed, but not worried, and his confidence set Rae's mind at ease. Just to make sure, he glanced back. "Rae, it takes an insane amount of concentration to do it. He couldn't keep it up if he was in trouble or something. He just wants some space."

She nodded quickly. Reassured, but having no intention whatsoever of giving him that space. "Thanks, Jules." She gestured to the lawn. "Looking good out there."

"Yeah," he snorted sarcastically, "the sling really helps."

"You'll be out of it soon." With a little wave, she started heading back inside to see if Molly had any idea where her missing boyfriend had made off to. But before she shut the door, Julian called out to her once more.

"Rae..." his voice softened, "you know we'll all be out of this soon. All of us."

Their eyes met and she forced a smile.

"I know we will."

He flashed a sad grin and shook his head. "You forget again..."

"I know..." she pushed open the door and headed inside, "...you know me."

Molly's room was actually just a few doors down from Rae's, and Rae had no doubt that she'd find her there. While she'd been delighted to see the rest of the PC and Knights mixed in and working together, Molly had been inexplicably determined to avoid such activities since they got to the compound. She certainly wouldn't be going out today.

That's why Rae was so surprised when she went inside.

Molly was dressed exactly like she was: head to toe black. Her crimson hair was swept up into a long ponytail, and when Rae came in she was just pulling on her old combat boots.

"Morning," she said briskly. The bed was still messy, and a plate of uneaten fruit was shoved into the far corner of her desk. But other than that, she looked like she was ready to go. A bit nervous, perhaps. But a bit of the old Molly coming back. A force to be reckoned with.

"Morning," Rae answered with scarcely contained delight. "Looks like someone woke up on the right side of the bed this—"

"I'm pregnant."

The world went black.

When Rae managed to open her eyes again, she was lying on her back. Molly's face floated over her, a mixture of concern and amusement all at the same time.

"Honestly, Kerrigan, only you would black out when I tell you that I'm—"

"You're pregnant?" Rae repeated in shock, sitting up and taking Molly's hands.

For a moment, Molly's determined show of force fractured, and a glimpse of the same bubbly girl who once set fire to her own ill-equipped closet leaked on through.

"Yeah, I am. About six weeks along." Her tiny shoulders trembled as she pulled in a shaky breath. "I found out...well, I found out the day we got here. Dr. Roscoe figured it out during my examination and told me when I woke up."

Rae brought her hands up to her mouth in shock. She couldn't even imagine. Waking up strapped to a bed in your enemy's infirmary—not knowing if the rest of your friends were alive or dead—only to learn that you and your boyfriend, who apparently lived here with his dad, who was apparently the chief, were expecting an unexpected child.

"Oh, Molls..."

What could she even say? She *could not* imagine. And even as she sat there, a thousand little things began to make sense.

"You didn't want to get involved in the politics or go back to Guilder," she said softly, piecing it together right there on the floor. "You didn't want to train."

"More than that," Molly whispered, "I didn't want to use my tatù. I didn't know whether it would hurt the baby. A thousand volts of electricity coursing through my body...what if I killed it?" A stream of steady tears slipped down her face, an expression mirrored quickly by Rae.

"You wanted me to sell the penthouse so you could have the money to buy a safe place for you and the baby. One that no one knew about."

Molly nodded bravely, but then she covered her face with her hands, sobbing. "Oh Rae, I didn't know how to tell you! I don't know how to tell Luke! I don't even know what I'm doing here! We had everything figured out and then we got fired, and shot at by our friends, and we didn't have jobs, and we ended up here, and Luke's dad turned out to be—" She lost her voice completely and started sobbing into her hands. "I don't know what to do!"

The next second, the two friends came together, wrapping their arms around each other as they rocked back and forth on the floor. Rae cried silently, overwhelmed for her friend, while Molly openly sobbed, burying her head in Rae's shoulder as a week's worth of terror and frustration came pouring out.

"I don't even know if it's a boy or a girl!" she finally choked. "I don't even know how I'm going to decorate the nursery!"

With a gasping laugh Rae pulled away, holding Molly at an arm's length as she looked her up and down. A fresh feeling of conviction surged through her, and with a steady smile she wiped her friend's cheeks and looked her squarely in the eyes. "You, Molly Skye, are going to be the world's best mother."

Molly's eyes locked onto hers, still swimming in tears. "Do you really think so?"

"There's not a doubt in my mind." On this point, Rae was certain. "We're going to keep you out of harm's way while we figure this whole mess out, and then, Molls, you're going to have the most perfect little baby on the planet. You and I will raise it together. Like we always planned. We'll move to Australia and become shepherds or something. Somewhere far away from here. The baby can play with the lambs. It'll look like a billboard for infant PETA."

A little giggle escaped Molly's lips and she leaned back against the bed, gathering together her thoughts as she slowed down her frantic breathing. "Too many snakes in Australia."

"Austria, then. They're spelled almost the same."

Another giggle. "It's a plan."

Rae smiled and squeezed her ankle. "Seriously, though...when are you going to tell Luke?"

"Today," Molly said suddenly. "Or tomorrow. Or maybe never. I haven't decided. Maybe I could just send him a postcard from Austria."

Rae nodded patiently. "Why don't we try...today?"

Molly bit her lip. She glanced fearfully out the window as the sounds of Luke and the training exercise filtered through. Then her hand drifted up to her stomach, and she cleared her face with sudden determination. "Tomorrow."

Rae hesitated, willing to support whatever she decided but trying to keep her on course. "Why tomorrow?"

In a blur of crimson and black, Molly got to her feet. "Because today I'm going to be training."

Rae scrambled up after her delighted, but anxious all at the same time. "Okay, well that's...but I mean, you have a point about your tatù. Are you sure it's—"

"Dr. Roscoe told me first thing that my ability won't affect my baby, especially because it's likely that my baby will have the same one. I've just been freaked about the idea."

A sudden image of a fire-bolt-wielding infant lit both of their faces with a smile.

"Maybe you should name it Zeus..." Rae said pensively.

Molly's eyes lit up. "I thought of that."

"At any rate," she paced a few steps forward and wrapped Molly up in another hug, "this is going to be one-hundred-percent okay. *Nothing* is going to happen to you or your kid. You guys are going to have a long, normal, boring life together. I promise."

"Thanks, Rae." Molly's voice was somewhat muffled in her waves of raven hair.

"And I'm proud of you."

She felt Molly smile. "Thanks."

With that, she swept towards the door like a woman on a mission, keeping a hand on her stomach and her eyes trained on the horizon. Rae watched her go with a secret smile. The surprises just kept coming, but this, at least, was something they could celebrate.

Molly was almost out the door when she turned around with a last, sudden fear.

"And..." her blue eyes widened like saucers, "and the nursery?"

"We can paint it yellow. Yellow is neutral."

"Right." She nodded to herself, taking more solace in this one tiny detail than in anything else. "It is."

The door swung shut behind her, leaving Rae feeling like she'd just experienced the entire range of human emotions all in a two-minute sitting. Leave it to Molly to do it all in one breath.

And leave it to Molly to rise above an impossible situation and come out on the other side even stronger. She'd seen Molly Skye do a number of inconceivable things over the years, but she didn't know if she had ever been so proud.

She was still smiling when she suddenly realized that she hadn't asked Molly the only question she'd come in here to say. Too late to do it now; it was hardly appropriate anyway, under the circumstances. She'd just have to find Devon the old-fashioned way.

As if on cue, her phone buzzed suddenly in her pocket. It was a text from Julian.

**Just got a read on Devon. He's back at the house.**

*Perfect! Then I'll just head over there and...*

Then Julian's words from before echoed suddenly through her mind: 'It takes an insane amount of concentration. He couldn't keep it up if he was in trouble.'

A chilling question wedged its way to the front of her brain.

*Why was Julian able to see him now?*

Rae didn't stop to answer any of a dozen greetings that were tossed her way as she raced across the lawn. She didn't stop to tell Julian that she was borrowing his car before she conjured up the keys and threw it into gear. She didn't stop at a single red light on her way back into the city.

Her mind was fixed on one thing and one thing only.

The chilling look on Devon's face as he'd carried her away from the school.

She double-parked in the middle of the street and rushed up the front steps like her life depended on it, pounding loudly at the door. When there was no answer, she kicked the damn thing in—flying through the living room before suddenly stopping cold. Her heart froze up in her chest as her eyes focused on a single thing.

An empty syringe lying on the floor.

And Devon's body lying beside it.

# Chapter 12

Rae didn't scream this time. There were no wasted words, no empty tears. When she looked back later, she thought that a part of her might have almost been expecting it.

"Devon," she gasped as she rushed to his side, shaking him gently. He winced a little in pain, but other than that his eyes stayed closed. "Devon, you've got to wake up."

Her eyes flicked from the empty needle lying on the floor, to the series of punctures and tiny bruises hidden in the crook of his arm.

"Sweetheart, *please*," she begged, tilting him up slightly so that his head was in her lap. "Please wake up for me."

Still nothing.

*How did this happen?! How did I let this happen?!*

Rae didn't need a doctor to tell her what was going on. She didn't need to be a genius to know that the syringe hadn't been full of penicillin or heroine. She knew exactly what was in the empty vial. She knew exactly what secret Devon had been keeping from her all this time.

Her hands flitted uselessly over him as she tried to think of what to do. Her first thought was to call an ambulance, but not even the Privy Council hospital would have any idea what to do. Her next thought was to call Carter, but what would he do besides sit here with her?

No. Devon had gotten himself into this mess. Devon would just have to pull himself out of it. And all Rae could do was sit here on the kitchen floor and hold his hand until that happened.

Seconds stretched into minutes and slowly stretched into a full hour.

Despite her resolution not to cry, a small river of tears had fallen down Rae's face. About five minutes in, she'd conjured him a blanket. His skin was icy cold, and even in his sleep he'd begun shivering. Five minutes after that, she took it back off again. A vicious fever settled upon him suddenly, flushing his body as a thin layer of sweat broke out over his forehead.

In the end all she could do was sit there and keep her fingers wrapped tightly around his wrist, monitoring his weak, sporadic pulse.

After what seemed like a small eternity, his hand twitched. His pulse sped up slightly as his forehead pulled together with a soft groan.

"Devon?" she whispered tentatively, squeezing his fingers.

He didn't reply. Maybe he couldn't. Maybe he couldn't even hear her. But his pulse quickened even more as his eyelids fluttered open and shut.

The second they were fully open, she hit him right in the face. Hard.

"Rae!" he gasped, bringing a shaking hand up to his cheek. "What are you—"

She smacked him again, ignoring the accompanying stab of guilt that followed when he turned his face protectively into her leg.

"What are you doing?" he groaned. "*Stop.*"

But Rae didn't stop. In fact, she didn't think she could even if she wanted to. The second he tried to gather himself together, she slapped him again.

"Come on! Enough!" he shouted, pushing away from her and shakily propping himself up against the wall. His arm came up half-heartedly as a shield in between them, but he was so depleted it only stayed there a few seconds before it dropped back down to his side.

"Tell me this isn't what I think it is."

His eyes opened tentatively and focused on the empty syringe she was holding in her hand.

If it was possible, his skin paled to an even scarier shade of white. His lips parted as he tried hopelessly to come up with something to say, but his usual quick retorts and denials fell short in the wake of utter exhaustion.

"Call a doctor," he finally pleaded, pressing his hands against his eyes and praying she would just forget the whole thing. "Call Alicia..."

"*No.*" Rae's voice was shaking as much as Devon's hands. But not with any kind of sickness. With a burning, all-consuming rage. "I'm guessing she wouldn't be able to do anything anyway. I'm guessing that's the reason you sent her away the last time. *For speaking in her mind!*"

She had always wondered why Alicia left so suddenly. Always wondered at the look that she and Devon had shared. Always wondered why, when Rae had first gotten there, he shrank away from her very touch. Now she knew.

It was because with every touch, he was absorbing another tatù.

And it was killing him.

In the silence that followed, they slowly met each other's eyes.

For a second, it looked like he was going to try to deny it. In his weakened state, Rae could practically see the rush of excuses parading through his mind. But one look at her face told him everything he needed to know. The jig was up.

"I took the vial of serum you found on Jennifer the day she was killed."

Rae said nothing. She knew it was the serum. She just wanted to hear him say it. Her chest rose and fell with quick, furious breaths, but she held her tongue. If only for the time being.

"When Kraigan took off that morning in Scotland, I saw a perfect opportunity and blamed it on him. But it wasn't him. It was me."

Rae balled her hands into fists. Half to prevent herself from reaching out and stroking the dark bruises painted beneath Devon's eyes. Half to prevent herself from lighting him on fire.

"I called up the professor from Oxford, the one we met in San Francisco. Got him to help me start taking it in small doses—studying the effects. At first, we thought it might be working, that I might be getting used to it. But then..." His voice trailed off as he wrapped his arms painfully around his chest. "He refused to keep helping me. Said he refused to watch."

"Refused to watch *what*?" Rae finally spoke, her soft voice simmering with an unbridled anger the likes of which she had never known. "Refused to watch you slowly kill yourself?"

Devon clenched his jaw. "It was *working*, Rae."

"It was KILLING you!"

Turns out the quiet voice hadn't lasted so long after all. She hurled the syringe down on the kitchen tile with all her might—shattering it into a million pieces.

"Do you have any more of it?" she demanded, unable to control her temper. His eyes flickered up in confusion. "Did you and the mad scientist make any more?"

"No," he said softly, gazing at the broken pieces with a hollow sort of look in his eyes. "That was it."

"I don't believe you!"

And she didn't. There was no longer any trust here. No reasonable expectation of certainty or given assumptions. For *months*—he had lied to her! And for *what*?!

His eyes turned to her for a split second, searching her face for any sort of compromise, before he cleared his expression with a simple shrug. "Not my problem."

*"Not your problem?!"*

A sudden feeling of weightlessness came over her, and Rae realized she had actually begun floating off the floor in rage. She switched quickly out of levitation and settled back on the tiles.

"Devon, what the hell are you—"

"You expect me to apologize?!" he demanded, rallying as best he could. He might not have the strength to raise his voice as loud as hers, but he made up for it with his eyes.

"IT WAS KILLING YOU!" she screamed again.

"NO!" He banged his fist down on the tile, oblivious to the fact that it was covered in shards of broken glass. "It was giving me the ONLY chance I had!"

"To do *what*?!" Rae refused to believe that the man she had given her heart to could be either so greedy or so stupid. "To become a superhero? Hate to break it to you, Devon, but you already have powers, and—"

"I HAVE ONE!"

A sudden stream of blood poured from his nose and he broke off, panting, as he leaned his body back against the wall. Rae wanted to say something, but she couldn't. She wanted to do something, but she couldn't. She just watched with wide, horrified eyes as the love of her life fell to pieces right in front of her.

"One power," he panted, cradling his bloody face, "against a man who has a thousand. One chance in a *thousand* to save the woman I love." He shook his head as desperate tears slid down his face, mixing in with the blood. "Rae, how am I supposed to stand next to you in this fight, just being what I am? I needed to be more! I needed to be more so I could protect you!"

Rae was trembling now just as much as him, hands braced against the tiles. "I am *not* letting you jump off any more cliffs for me!"

"Open your eyes, Rae!" he shouted. "We're already there!"

With that—he broke off coughing, half slumping forward as he reached out for a table leg to steady himself. Rae caught his hand instead, holding him upright as she conjured a damp cloth and began gently wiping the blood from his face.

*...and that's why I love him.*

Greedy? Stupid? Had she really considered those things? That Devon would do something like this—try to gather the world's powers—for any kind of self-glory? Of *course* he was doing it for her. Of *course* he was doing it to beat back the man who was trying to do her harm. Of *course* he hadn't even considered the personal cost before throwing his body in between her and danger.

Shooting up with lethal chemicals, hurling his body between her and a hundred gunmen, throwing himself off a cliff.

To Devon, it was all the same thing.

It was all loving her.

"I saw Cromfield yesterday afternoon. In the park, right outside here."

He caught his breath and pulled back in alarm, eyes automatically checking her over for any signs of damage. "Why didn't you—" he broke off coughing, "why didn't you tell me?!"

"It all happened really fast," she said quietly, still dabbing at his face. When she was finished, she picked up his hand and began gently pulling out little slivers of glass. "All he wanted to do was talk. He stuck me with some of Angel's blood to make sure that's all that would happen."

Devon's whole face crumbled. "Rae...shit! I'm so sorry. I should have been there. You should never have been there alone."

"He told me he wouldn't kill anyone I cared about," she continued abruptly. "He said that he wouldn't touch a hair on their head—as long as I went with him and no one stood in our way."

Devon stopped breathing, staring at her like his life depended on it. When he finally spoke, his voice was no more than a whisper. "What did you say?"

Rae set his hand down, and stared intently up into his eyes. "I told him no."

Granted, she hadn't been able to say so out loud. But there were no delusions between them that she had any intention of going along with his plan. Not now. Not ever.

Devon's shoulders fell as he visibly exhaled. "You did? I mean—of course you did."

Rae shook her head. "There's no 'of course' about it. Do you want to know what I would have said if I was you? *Yes.*"

"That's not—"

"It *is* true, Devon. That's exactly what would have happened. You would have said yes; you would have said or done anything you could just to keep me alive." She shook her head, staring deep into his eyes. "Here I was, handed a literal 'Devon-walks-away-free' card, and I threw it back in his face. Now why do you think I did that? Do you think it's because I love you less than you love me?"

He bit his lip and stayed silent, caught in the inescapable implications of her words.

"Don't you get it? This is *real.*" She gestured between them. "You and me. That's *real.* So you can't be so quick to get yourself killed. You can't go throwing yourself in front of buses, or sampling Molly's cooking, or messing around with chemicals you don't understand. You need to keep yourself alive—so I can be with you. That's all I want. That's the only thing that will make me happy."

When he still didn't say anything, she poked at his knee with a tentative smile.

"You want to make me happy, don't you?"

His tortured face softened into a tender smile. "You have no idea how much I want that."

"I don't want you to be my bodyguard, Devon. I want you to be my boyfriend." A sudden blush rose up in her cheeks, and she dropped her eyes to the ground. "And on that point, I'm afraid I'll require nothing less than perfection."

A chorus of soft laughter lightened the heavy mood.

Without another word, she took him delicately by the wrists and helped him up to his feet. He was still a bit unsteady, but after a moment he was able to stand there on his own. She bent down to pick up their phones, both of which had fallen out during their standoff, but before she could he reached out and took her gently by the hands.

"What is it?" she asked curiously, glancing between him and the mess on the floor. She'd have to conjure a broom and get this glass swept away before someone—

"Rae..."

Her head snapped up as her heart skipped a nervous beat in her chest. There was something very strange in his voice. Something she had never quite heard there before.

As she was trying to figure it out, he stared into her searching eyes—looking more than a little nervous himself. For a second it looked like he was about to back out entirely. Then he swallowed hard and squeezed her hands with a little smile.

"I didn't forget your birthday, Rae."

She blinked. That was not at all what she'd been expecting him to say.

"Oh, well," she tried to recover herself, "it doesn't really matter anyway."

"No, it does matter." He pulled in a shaky breath. "Carter never asked me to—"

A shrill ring shattered the air between them. In perfect unison, they lowered their eyes to where Rae's phone was rattling away on the ground. A moment later, Devon's phone joined it.

She shook her head with a grin, before glancing back up. "Saved by the bell, huh?"

Devon looked like he'd been punched in the gut. "...Yeah."

Without another thought, Rae reached down and answered, tossing Devon his at the same time. It was Gabriel.

"Hey, you need to get back here," he said with no further preamble. "Keene called and the whole lot of us is headed back to Guilder. Apparently, they've reached some sort of decision."

Rae glanced over at Devon as Julian's voice leaked through his phone. Judging by Devon's expression, he was getting the exact same message as her.

"We'll meet you at the school," she said quickly. "We're in the city—so we'll get there in about an hour."

"Hurry."

Without another word, Gabriel hung up. Rae was still mulling this over when Julian asked some sort of question, and Devon glanced up at her with a curious grin.

'Did you borrow Jules' car?' he mouthed silently.

Rae's face paled at the exact moment she heard the tow-truck pulling away from the house.

*Oh shit... Two cars in two days... I don't know who's going to strangle me first.*

With a look of supreme innocence, she shook her head, eyes flicking out the blinds to where Julian's Jaguar was vanishing slowly down the street. A second later, Devon hung up.

"So... back off to Guilder then?"

She pulled in a deep breath, watching the taillights disappear. "Yeah. Hopefully it's for some good news this time." As they headed outside, she glanced suddenly over at him. "Hey—what was that you were trying to tell me? Before the call?"

His breathing hitched for a second, before he said, "Oh...nothing. It can wait." With a casual smile, he tossed her his keys. "Think it's probably best if you drive us there."

She eyed his ashen skin before glancing wistfully down the road. "You'd be surprised."

Without another word, they piled into the car. Ready to head once more into the breach.

"Dev?"

"Yeah?"

"...how much does a Jaguar cost?"

The drive from London to Guilder was a bit faster than the one from the Abbey to Guilder, so Rae and Devon got there was a little time to spare. It was an abruptly odd moment. Rae couldn't remember how many times the two of them had breezed through these gates into the parking lot. Now, not only was she uncertain as to whether or not they'd be shot upon entering, but the gate itself had been ripped right out of the ground.

Devon parked on the side of the driveway and the two of them sat silently in the front seat, gazing incredulously at the thick, uprooted stone.

"How could he have possibly done that?" Devon asked quietly.

Rae shook her head—trying to imagine a tatù that would do it. "I don't know."

A couple minutes later, they heard the sound of tires and looked back to see a black line of cars proceeding slowly up the gravel path. Fodder nodded at them from the front seat as he passed, and the two of them fell into line behind the others.

After they'd finally parked and people began spilling from the cars, Rae spotted Luke and Molly from across the lot. While everyone else was rigid with attention, marching down to the Oratory with a shared look of concern, the two of them were in their own little world.

Luke was beaming like a miniature sun while Molly was resting her head lightly against his shoulder, the two of them strolling hand-in-hand down the shaded path. As they walked in front of Rae, the little redhead shot her a secret wink.

Rae bit down on her own lip to keep from grinning like a fool, trying to keep her mind focused on the task at hand instead. Molly would tell the rest of the world when she was ready. By the looks of it, Luke couldn't have been more thrilled with the news, so for now everyone else could wait. They had a peace plan to negotiate first. And a whole mess of people to save.

Louis Keene came out to meet them the second they rounded the corner. Rae couldn't tell whether that was a good thing or not. He was flanked by a pair of men, and the guy already looked like he could handle himself. But Carter held out his hand with a warm smile, a smile that Keene reciprocated in full before gesturing him and Fodder inside.

"And Miss Kerrigan," he added suddenly, causing Rae to startle in surprise. "You and your friends have been more instrumental than anyone else in facilitating this change. Won't you all join us, please?"

She and Devon shared a quick look before glancing at the rest of the gang. They looked as hesitant as she was. What if there were more gunmen waiting just on the other side of the Oratory doors? But, again, Carter cleared his throat pointedly and they filed in obediently., down through the large training room, then through the underground halls that lead them to the PC training center and into a large room.

As they settled around the familiar oval table—in a room that Rae had been in a hundred times for debriefings—she cast a tentative glance at Fodder. Sure enough, he was staring around the room with a touch of surprise, probably as struck by the uncanny similarities between here and the war room at the Abbey as she had been her first time there. Her lips curved up in a little smile as she settled back in her chair to listen to what she hoped would be the new world order.

"First of all—I want to apologize for how things were handled last night," Keene began diplomatically. "The sight of Mallins' body...it sent people into a panic. But an execution on the lawn by firing squad?" He shook his head. "Miss Kerrigan, you have my sincerest apologies. I assure you, the men in question have been dealt with accordingly."

Rae nodded quickly as Devon stiffened automatically by her side. "Uh...thank you, sir."

Keene flashed a smile. "With that being said, I'd like to go right ahead and tell you what we've learned. To start—Cromfield didn't kill Mallins. The president killed himself."

There was a sudden burst of conversation around the table, but Rae leaned back in her chair in silent shock.

*He killed himself. That means...Cromfield didn't get the tatù. So, there might still be a chance—*

"Rae?"

Rae glanced up to see Carter as well as the rest of the table looking at her expectantly. Her skin flushed as she looked towards her future stepfather, sensing she had missed a question.

"I'm sorry—what was that?"

Carter's face softened. "Acting-President Keene was just expressing his confusion over Mr. Mallins' suicide. We all know Cromfield is collecting powers, but Mallins was only telekinetic. A useful gift to be sure, but hardly a rare one. Do you have any idea why he would take his own life?"

He stared intently into her eyes, and for a moment the entire room paused.

Rae stared back, at a temporary loss for words.

Carter was leaving it up to her to expose Mallins or not, as she saw fit. It was fair, she supposed. She had been wronged the most, so the decision was up to her. But still...it was a grave responsibility.

"Actually—" she began, but something made her pause.

*He might have been a monster, but Mallins gave his final breath to keep us safe. The least I can do is keep his secret.*

She cleared her throat and glanced down at her lap. "Actually, I have no idea, sir."

Carter's eyes flashed, and for a moment he looked profoundly proud. Then he turned back to Keene—business as usual. "So,

Mr. Keene. As acting-president, what is it the Council has decided to do?"

Keene glanced at his counselors, before shaking his head. "You'd have to ask them yourself. You see, my first order of business as acting-president...is stepping down as acting-president."

There was a small gasp from the Knights' side of the table, but the PC looked calm and certain. Only Carter was at a loss.

"Louis," he urged quietly, "now is no time to divide the ranks with some kind of vote for your successor. We need to move on Cromfield *now*. Time is of the essence!"

Keene regarded him calmly. "Oh, there's not going to be a vote. We did the vote already, you see. At the end of our last meeting last night. My successor has already been unanimously voted into place."

Carter threw up his hands. "Then who the hell should I be talking to right now?"

Keene smiled. "You."

This time, the PC reaction was just as strong as the Knights—a table's worth of people expressing their support and united agreement.

Only Carter remained on the fence. "Louis...this isn't what—"

"I never wanted this, Andrew," Keene cut him off. "I lost the vote to keep you here, and then I was forced into it when you left. You know what to do with these people, and you know how to handle Cromfield a hell of a lot better than I ever could. I will, however, offer my services to assist you in whatever way I can."

Carter looked as though he was about to refuse, but this time it was Rae who cleared her throat sharply. The entire table chuckled appreciatively as he gave her a look of exasperation.

"Fine," he conceded. "For at least the time being, I would be honored to steer us through this transition. Granted, that you agree with what I have to propose."

Rae and her friends leaned forward in their seats. Here it was...

"The time for the Privy Council to discard some of its more antiquated traditions is long overdue. It's time for us to cast aside the heavy burden of needless secrecy and the lines of division that follow. From this day forward, every student at Guilder and every agent on the Council is free to tell whomever they deem appropriate about their abilities. Everyone they love. Everyone they trust. As long as these people can be sworn to secrecy themselves, there's no need for the rest of us to live in perpetual isolation."

A controlled explosion followed this statement as a whole new world of possibilities opened its door. As Rae glanced around the table, she could see the surreal excitement of it dancing in her friends' eyes. Sons could finally tell their mothers. Daughters could finally tell their fathers. Entire families would be brought together tonight.

But Carter wasn't finished. As he stared around the table, he made sure that everyone seated there looked up and met his eyes. "My reasons for saying this are two-fold. The first you just heard and the second is this: If we are to weather the storm that is coming, we are going to need all hands on deck. Young and old. Inked and not. Hybrid...or otherwise. We must all unite together, or we will fall."

A silent gasp caught in Rae's throat and she realized she had tears in her eyes. She shifted in her seat to wipe them discreetly on her sleeve, but even as she was doing so Carter called her name.

"Miss Kerrigan." His voice rang out over the table as he locked onto her with a singular smile. "All hands on deck. What does that mean?"

A feeling of indescribable warmth spread through Rae's entire body as her eyes glowed with a long-awaited victory.

"Take us to the dungeons."

# Chapter 13

"I'm not sure this is the best idea," Keene murmured, holding his hand even higher to light the way down the darkened corridor. Six of them were heading to the prison cells, similar to the one Rae had been in not too long ago. Others behind Keene were carrying cell phones, some carrying torches, depending on the age bracket. Keene was carrying what looked to be a handful of liquid lava, but Rae had a sneaking suspicion that had something to do with his tatù.

She followed silently, originally not sure that the PC actually had hybrids in prison, and then as they followed Keene, she grew more and more anxious. Someone like Mallins could have easily taken a hybrid and hidden them in this dark hole. The president of the PC could have offered them a job—students left Guilder before graduation all the time—and no one thought anything of it. She was the only hybrid she knew of while she attended Guilder, besides Kraigan, but... could there have been more? Could Carter have known and let this happen? Could the ones down in the cells all be dangerous? She shuddered, not wanting to think too long about it.

Carter followed closely by Keene's side, along with Fodder. "We agreed we needed everyone. The people down here are the ones likely to be of the most use in the battle to come."

"Yeah," Keene muttered, approaching the first door, "but they're also likely to be the ones most likely to battle us first," he shook his head. "And they have every right."

Rae exchanged a look with Devon, her eyes flashing in the dark. He was holding his cellphone up to light the inscription carved out above the door.

'A2LHI4.'

She blinked in disgust. They didn't even have names?

"When I open it up, let me do all the talking," Carter instructed softly.

The only people down in the giant stone cavern were him, Keene, Fodder, Rae, and Devon. They were joined by one of Fodder's men to balance them out. It had taken over twenty minutes speed-walking beneath the foundation of the school just to get there, and no matter how quietly Carter spoke, the sound of it echoed back a thousand times.

"You also might want to switch out of your fox tatù," Carter added, sensing her distress. He shot a sideways glance at her boyfriend. "Sorry, Devon."

Devon shook his head dismissively, and Rae suspected that he was just grateful to be dealing with only one set of ink at the moment.

"So who is this?" Fodder asked carefully, similarly struck by the carving on the door.

Carter looked up with a sigh. "This is Harriet Mills. Father had the ability to manipulate water molecules, mother had the ability to create electricity—very much like Miss Skye. When she was first gifted with the ink, the combination proved deadly—killing two agents and a member of the Guilder teaching staff who was trying to help her."

The group of them took a small step back as he searched for the correct key.

"So you locked her up for that?" Rae demanded incredulously. "Water and electricity—no one could control that. It wasn't her fault. You locked her up in there with all that guilt?"

"Not me, Rae, no." Carter sighed as he selected the correct one. "In fact, since I was named president, I made repeated efforts to see those who were wrongfully incarcerated set free. I was voted down every time. A certain member of the Council kept a handful of key votes in his pocket."

Devon folded his arms across his chest and stared down the darkened cavern with a shudder. "And who was that?"

Carter glanced behind him before springing the lock free. "Victor Mallins."

The door swung slowly open with a low *creeeeak*, groaning under the weight of years of rust and disuse. The six of them peered tentatively into the darkness—lifting their phones.

"Harriet?" Carter called cautiously. "My name is Andrew Carter. I work for the Privy Council. We've come to set you—"

Rae's hand whipped out and caught the bolt of white hot lightning before it could strike him through the heart. Slipping into Molly's tatù, she absorbed it simultaneously, wringing her fingers to shake of the burning sizzle in her hand.

Both Carter and Fodder turned to her in silent shock. They exchanged quick glances before Carter cleared his throat briskly. "Nice catch."

Devon rolled his eyes while Rae stifled a grin. "What are daughters for?"

The six of them peered into the darkness once more, banding a bit closer together as they waited for a response. This time a woman ventured forth, hands raised in front of her.

"Where's Avery?" she demanded in a shrill voice, eyes darting frantically between them. She flinched as Carter took a pacifying step. "Where's President Avery?"

"Harriet," he said calmly, "I'm President Carter. Wilson Avery died three years ago—and retired long before that. My associates and I represent the new Council, along with a contingent from the Xavier Knights. We've come to get you out of here."

Rae couldn't tell how much of this she was absorbing, and how much was lost in years of shock. Whatever the case, Harriet certainly wasn't reassured, that much was sure. She kept her hands raised in between them like a shield, fingers flickering occasionally like Molly's did when she got angry or nervous.

"I want to speak to Avery," she said again, unable to believe that this wasn't some sort of trick. "I have rights, you know. I can't be kept in here indefinitely without so much as a trial—"

"Harriet..."

Ignoring the fierce look of warning from Carter and the equaled look of exasperation from Devon, Rae stepped slowly forward. The woman watched her carefully. Growing up in the world of tatùs, you learned not to judge someone's capacity based on just their age. She kept her eyes trained on Rae's face, until Rae decided to do something that was both very trusting, and very stupid.

After sucking in a deep breath, she turned slowly around.

"Rae! What the hell are you doing?" Devon hissed, his face alight with fear.

But she calmly shook her head. "It's okay." Then a little louder to Harriet, "It's okay. You see? I'm just like you." Offering a silent prayer that now wasn't the moment Harriet might decide to shoot more lightning, Rae lifted up the bottom of her shirt. She heard Harriet's gasp behind her as she saw the glistening fairy—a tatù like no other before it. There was the soft padding of footsteps, and the next moment Rae felt a pair of cold fingertips graze her lower back.

"You're a hybrid," came a rough whisper from behind her.

"Yes." Rae turned around with a huge smile. "Just like you. And it's time to get you out of here."

They opened the rest of the cells together, one by one, their little band growing bigger with every door they unlocked. Most of the reactions went the same way as Harriet. There would be a warning shot or two—justifiably so—followed by a demonstration of trust and solidarity on Rae's part, which ended up bringing most of them around.

It was actually easier than she thought it would be. Most of them were so frightened of their own powers that they'd actually welcomed some level of isolation. And even those who were forcibly imprisoned understood that the people responsible for putting them there were long gone.

There were one or two who could not be persuaded. Who had been down in the darkness for too long and had resigned themselves to it. From these, Rae got an earful of profanities the likes of which she'd never heard, as well as a burning spray of what looked to be green slime.

She was still wringing it from her sleeve with a look of disgust, when Devon came up behind her and kissed her on the cheek. "I'm really proud of you," he murmured into her ear. "Walking into all these cells like you're doing. Showing them you trust them by showing them your ink."

Rae flung the remaining drops of slime from her fingertips. "Hey, I'm just glad I didn't wear a dress today, or this whole show and tell thing really could have gone the other way."

He was still chuckling as they came to a stop in front of the last door. This one looked a bit more foreboding than the rest— set apart at the end of its own hall in complete and utter isolation. An extra hedge of stone had been built up around it, and, unlike its counterparts, there was no inscription written above the door.

Carter stared up at it with a look of confusion before glancing down at his papers. "I don't understand," he murmured. "There's no record of this ever being in use... Louis, do you have any record of this?"

Keene shook his head. "I was told the last cell on the level belonged to Thomas." He gestured behind him to a man who was cheerfully conjuring what looked like giant bubbles.

Carter turned back to the door, looking a bit hesitant to discover who or what was inside.

"I'll open it," Rae volunteered, swallowing hard. This room was meant to be a secret. Maybe someone like her was imprisoned behind these walls. Her offering to open it would give Carter a way to save face with the others, not to mention the fact that Carter's ability was in no way defensive. Whatever firepower was in there, he'd have no way to protect himself.

"Mallins must have locked someone in here without anyone's knowledge." He glanced at Keene before pressing his lips tightly together and turned to Rae. "Thank you, Rae, but I've...I've got it." He stepped bravely forward, but both Fodder and Keene caught his arm at the same time.

"Let her do it," Fodder instructed, tossing Rae a little wink. "Better her than us."

"Thanks," she said frostily, but she returned the wink to Fodder. "Just remember, though, Kerrigan paybacks can be a deadly." She smiled when his face faltered and he hesitated. "I'm kidding," she told him.

Everyone stood in front of the door as Carter handed her the keys. She played with a few, trying to calm the shaking inside of her, hoping she appeared collected on the outside. She heard the other hybrids murmur worriedly behind her. On the third key, she heard the distinctive click that it was the correct one. She hesitated a mere second.

"Be careful, Rae," Devon murmured, coming to stand by her side and ready to protect.

Rae took a deep breath and turned the key in the lock. "Step back, everyone. Please." She readied herself, her tatù understanding the signals her brain was sending as it jumped from tatù to tatù, trying to figure what ability would be the strongest to use.

She unlocked the door and held her breath as she pulled open the heavy door. She braced herself for some bolt of attack, and stepped forward hesitantly when nothing happened immediately.

All the air was sucked out of her lungs as a man ventured out of the darkness, eyes glowing in the torchlight like some sort of predatory beast. His chest heaved as anger covered his features. A man to whom she bore an uncanny resemblance.

Her jaw dropped in shock as her phone clattered to the floor.

*"Kraigan?"*

# Chapter 14

There was a beat of silence. A frozen moment where no one seemed to know what to do.

Brother looked at sister. Sister looked at brother.

But then her brother looked at the man he believed was responsible for locking him up. *"You're a freakin' dead man!"* he roared as he flew past Rae, sending her flying into the wall. She hit the stone with a sharp crack and a painful scream, clutching at her stomach as she crumbled to the ground.

The scream was most likely the only thing that saved Carter's life.

The second he heard it, Kraigan froze in his tracks, looking back at Rae like he didn't think she was capable of making that kind of sound. When she didn't get up off the floor, he ventured cautiously back and bent close to her, as if she was playing some sort of prank. "What the hell happened to you? Why are you acting like this?"

"She got stabbed, you son of a bitch!" Devon growled, crouching down beside her. "Honey, are you okay?"

"Stabbed..." Kraigan shoved Devon aside with complete disregard, torchlight flickering in his eyes as he focused on his older sister. "Where the hell is he?"

"Who?" Rae panted, clutching at her sides.

A strange emotion flitted across Kraigan's face. One Rae was willing to bet he was feeling for the first time. He looked almost...protective.

"The man who did this to you," he snarled. "Where the hell is he?"

"Dead, I'm afraid. Apparently took his own life," Carter answered, surprisingly calm considering two seconds ago he was about to be ripped in half.

"You'll get your turn, president!" Kraigan warned before turning back to Rae. "I'm serious, where is he? We'll hunt him down together."

"The president's right." She winced as she pushed herself cautiously to her feet. "He's dead. And he was the guy who locked you up in here—not Carter." Kraigan's eyes flashed murderously behind Rae, and she put a cautious hand on his arm. "Kraigan, really. Mallins put you in here. Carter didn't know. Neither did with the rest of us. We had no idea you were in here. If we did, I'd have come a lot sooner. I'm so sorry." Tears threatened to fall. "I'm didn't know. I'm so sorry." She angrily swiped at an escaped tear, ignoring the pain shooting across her abdomen. "How long? Did they hurt you? They didn't give you needles or serum or anything, did they? I'll kill 'em. If there are any more involved in this... in this... crap!" She gasped and tried to catch her breath, not sure what to say.

A year ago, Kraigan would have laughed in her face. But as it stood, he just gave her a measured stare before nodding slowly. His eyes then flicked over the curious crowd behind them before his lips turned up in a wicked smirk.

"So these are the other residents of Cell Block D, are they? Tell me..." his eyes narrowed as he stared around the group, "which of you is the one who always sings..."

As Thomas, the unfortunate bubble-maker, shrank back into the shadows, Rae grabbed Kraigan's arm and started pulling him back up through the cavern.

"Come, brother," she said quietly, but not before switching to a tatù she knew she didn't need—just to be safe. "Let's get you back into the sun."

Kraigan explained as they walked that he hadn't made it more than forty-eight hours after he took off from the farm in Scotland before he was captured. He had actually been intending to go back—or so he said—when he popped up on a surveillance feed, and the next thing he knew a dozen or more agents had him surrounded.

"I could have gotten away," he boasted again through a mouthful of ribs.

The second they were back in the city he'd insisted upon eating a 'proper meal' instead of 'that bloody awful prison shit.' To Kraigan, a proper meal apparently consisted of an entire side of beef. An idea Devon wasn't entirely opposed to, but the savage way Kraigan was tearing through the bones was bound to give Rae nightmares.

"Even with Devon's lame tatù, I still could have gotten away." He poured an extra helping of barbeque sauce on his plate. "Except they threw this kid at me."

"I'm sorry..." Rae raised her eyebrows, "they threw a kid at you?" *Interesting tactic.* Although she wouldn't have counted on Kraigan to flinch.

Kraigan rolled his eyes. "Some rookie—fresh out of the academy."

"A rookie," Devon repeated with obvious delight, taking a swig of beer. "You got taken down by a rookie?"

Kraigan practically bared his teeth. "It wasn't how it sounds. It's not like he fought me or anything. I just...I accidently took his power."

With a look of disgust, Rae leaned forward with a napkin and tried to wipe a drip of sauce off of his chin. "And what was his power?"

He slapped away her hand and swiped Devon's beer at the same time. "He's a healer."

The irony was almost too much.

"A *what*?!" Rae demanded, grinning from ear to ear.

Kraigan shot her a sour look. "I know. It wasn't lost on me. I'm guessing that's why they picked him. They knew I'd steal it."

"Well, let that be a lesson to you," Devon declared smugly. He still hadn't gotten over the fact that it had been his tatù Kraigan had made off with. "You shouldn't take things without asking first."

Kraigan glared at him and angrily bit into another rib.

Molly, still giving him a hard time about tripping so many times up the stairs, added, "Maybe a little time in isolation was exactly what you needed."

Kraigan set down his ribs with a rather frightening smile. "Hey, Dev." He leaned forward across the table, reaching for Devon's head. "You've got something on your face, let me just—"

"Oh, fuck that!" Devon leapt back so fast he almost knocked their drinks clean off the table. "There's no way in hell you're touching me again. *Ever.* You can keep your awesome healing ink."

"Actually, I'll take it!" Rae said suddenly. Imagine all the times she could have used something like that if it had been in her arsenal. This afternoon being a prime example. At the rate they were going, it was bound to become one of her favorites. "I'll trade you something for it."

"Really?" Kraigan lit up for the first time. "Whatcha got?"

"How about Devon's?" Rae grinned slyly. "Since you liked it so much before."

Brother and sister shared a rare smile as Devon fumed in the corner.

"Absolutely not!" he exclaimed.

"Why not?" Rae asked innocently. "It's not like you'll be losing it—just me. And I can pick it back up from you again the second it's gone."

"It's just..." he spluttered as he looked between them, outraged that they were on the same side, "...it's the principle of the thing. I don't want him to have it."

"Dev," Rae said chidingly, offering Kraigan her hand, "let's show a little maturity, shall we? I think it's great progress that Kraigan didn't just take it himself—he was waiting for permission."

Kraigan's face blanked. "Actually, I was just waiting until after I ate..."

Rae ignored this, wrapping her fingers around his wrist.

The effect was instantaneous, sweeping through both of them at once. In a flash, she was able to pick up his healing tatù, while at the same time he extracted the fox from her. They pulled away a second later, each a little smug—like two kids who both thought they'd made the better trade on the playground.

With an apologetic smile, Rae turned to Devon next. "Sorry, babe. Do you think I could...?"

She reached out to stroke his face, but he leaned petulantly away, glaring out the window instead while Kraigan gleefully finished his beer. "No. You may not," Devon sputtered.

She hesitated. "You know I don't like to do these things without consent."

On the other side of the table, Kraigan rolled his eyes before launching into another set of ribs. "Just get on with it already— this is like a bad PSA."

"Devon..." she leaned forward with a seductive smile, tilting her face up to his, "if I promise not to mimic your tatù, will you give me a kiss?"

The corners of his lips turned up, but he tried to hold his ground. "Just a kiss?"

"That's all, I promise."

Kraigan scowled darkly. "Do not do that in front of me. I just got out of prison. Do you think I need that image burned into my—*oh, come on!*"

But it was too late. With a gigantic smile, Devon pulled Rae the rest of the way in, sweeping his hand behind her hair as their lips came together.

The second they were touching, she stole his tatù as they both knew she would—promises be damned. He chuckled softly as he felt it lift lightly from his body, but pulled her in with a new strength, knowing she could match it now as the ink flowed fresh through her skin.

They didn't stop until Kraigan cut short their bliss with a perfectly timed: "So where exactly is the bastard Cromfield?"

*Way to ruin the moment...*

They pulled apart with identical scowls, which they directed full-force at Kraigan. The guy couldn't have cared less. He simply stared between them expectantly, a pile of bones on his plate.

While Devon ordered another round of drinks, Rae leaned forward with a sigh. "We don't know exactly where he is now, but we have a tracker on our team, just waiting to be prepped. We know he's close." She swallowed. "I talked with him yesterday in London."

"What does he want?" Kraigan asked curiously, licking the sauce from his fingers. Only he wouldn't bother to ask why she had talked and not fought.

Rae hesitated. These were exactly the sorts of details they had bent over backwards to keep out of Kraigan's hands. Whatever progress he had made, the boy was still a walking, talking sociopath, and there was really no predicting what he would do in an explosive situation such as this.

*If we are to weather this storm, we must unite.*

Carter's words echoed in her head, and she leaned back with a little sigh. Whether Kraigan was ready to hear it or not...it was time.


"Well, he sure hopped on board fast."

Rae walked up to Devon through the tall grass, her long dress swishing back and forth in the gentle Scottish breeze. They had arrived at her mother's farmhouse earlier that afternoon, and they most certainly had not been alone. If her mother was surprised to see twenty or more members of the Knights and Privy Council arrive at her doorstep, she certainly didn't say so. She just kissed Rae on the cheek and opened the door wider with a cursory, "There's lunch on the stove."

The Abbey was safe house number one. Guilder was safe house number two. And upon Rae's urging, it had been decided that the farmhouse would be safe house number three.

For one thing—Cromfield didn't know where it was. They couldn't say as much for the other two. And while Guilder and the Abbey were great centers for operation, they didn't exactly feel like home. Not like Scotland did.

No, the farmhouse was the place to be. They had already used it as a training center once. They could do it again. It could be a more intimate center for operations. A launching point as people from every agency and rank set out across the globe to gather together all the tatùs that they could find. Men and women alike. Children and parents. Hybrids.

Thanks to the looming threat of Cromfield, Rae and her friends were preparing for the greatest coming together of tatùs the world had ever seen. Never before in history would there be gathered together so many people with ink. It would be a revolutionary affair. A new world precedent. One that was likely to shape the history of their people for generations to come.

"Yeah, well, we both guessed that was going to happen. The kid's insane."

Devon laced his fingers with hers as she came to stand beside him on the cliff. At his request, they had driven away from the commotion at the house for a few hours, to watch the sunset over the high ocean cliffs. The salt air misted up around them as a glorious swirl of vibrant gold and fiery crimson painted the sky. It reminded Rae of the cliffs over at Dunnett Head, the ones where she'd found her father's note. She remembered standing there all by herself, thinking it was the most beautiful thing she'd ever seen.

This moment might top that.

And that might have a lot to do with the man standing beside her. Or everything.

She smiled to herself as she rested her head lightly on his shoulder.

What a year it had been. And what was yet to come. Her world was spinning at such a pace that she couldn't even begin to wrap her mind around it. It was all she could do to hang on for dear life, and pray she was still standing when it was all over.

And yet, she had this nagging suspicion that someone here was going to make sure she was.

"What're you thinking about?" she asked softly, peering up at Devon's face.

He smiled down at her for a second before answering simply, "You."

She smiled to herself and stared out over the waves, squeezing his hand tighter in hers. "It's so beautiful," she murmured. "I can hardly catch my breath."

"Me neither," he replied thoughtfully. "It's one of the reasons I wanted to bring you out here, to show you..."

She peered down over the edge of the bluff to the crashing waves below. "Perhaps you forgot," she teased, "I specifically asked you *not* to jump off any more cliffs."

He laughed softly and lifted his eyes to the horizon. "Actually...I was thinking about jumping off the biggest one of all."

She looked up curiously. "I'm not sure I know what you mean."

A flash of fear passed across his face, replaced with a look Rae had never seen before. "Rae, I didn't forget your birthday. And Carter didn't ask me to go away with him. I needed some time...to get you a present."

The wind stirred her hair around her as she searched his eyes, wondering what was going on in that beautiful head of his. "Okay...well, do you have it here? Or should we go back to the..."

He sank down onto one knee.

*Wait! What? What...is happening?*

Time seemed to stop as she looked down at him through a windswept tangle of raven-colored curls, frozen in surprise and haloed in sunlight.

His eyes twinkled as he reached down into his pocket. "Rae Kerrigan," he took a second to catch his breath, "from the moment I tackled you on the first day of school, I haven't been able to get you out of my head. From that day on, I've carried you with me wherever I go. You've changed my world, Rae. Brightened it in a way I didn't know was possible. Turned it upside-down and inside out, and made it something worth living."

With trembling fingers, he opened the little box. "I love you more than life itself. I always have, and I always will."

An exquisite diamond sparkled in the air between them.

"Will you marry me?"

**THE END**
**Coming June 2016**

# DESCRIPTION

*Rae of Light is the 12th Book of W.J. May's bestselling series, The Chronicles of Kerrigan.*

It's time to face the music—except there is no music, just a low warning of a war that is to come. There are no other options but to confront Cromfield. No more running, no more hiding. Rae Kerrigan will be forced into an eternal life sentence if they do not stop him.

Except, how do you stop a madman that cannot die? How do you risk the lives of everyone you love, your family, friends and the lives of innocent people? Rae is running out of time and possibilities.

Will the sins of the father be the sins of the daughter?

It's up to Rae to find a way to undo the dark evil in her family's past to have a ray of hope for everyone's future.

# Note from Author

*I stare at these pages and wonder where the years have gone. It's not that many, lol, but it seems the idea of Rae and her tatù started forming in my head just a little bit ago. Now, here we are, 11 books later and on the eve of the final book for Rae...*

*However, I have to admit that I don't feel this story is over. I'm excited to start the prequel and let readers know what I've know all along about Simon and Beth. And then... will there be more for Rae? That's for the readers to decide! You tell me if you want more Rae, Devon & the gang adventures!*

*All the best, W.J. May*

**Newsletter:** http://eepurl.com/97aYf
**Website:** http://www.wanitamay.yolasite.com
**Facebook:** https://www.facebook.com/pages/Author-WJ-May-FAN-PAGE/141170442608149

# The Chronicles of Kerrigan

# CoK Prequel!

A Novella of the Chronicles of Kerrigan.
A prequel on how Simon Kerrigan met Beth!!
NOW AVAILABLE:

# More books by W.J. May

## Hidden Secrets Saga:
### Download Seventh Mark part 1 For FREE
### Book Trailer:
http://www.youtube.com/watch?v=Y-_yVYClgvo

Like most teenagers, Rouge is trying to figure out who she is and what she wants to be. With little knowledge about her past, she has questions but has never tried to find the answers. Everything changes when she befriends a strangely intoxicating family. Siblings Grace and Michael, appear to have secrets which seem connected to Rouge. Her hunch is confirmed when a horrible incident occurs at an outdoor party. Rouge may be the only one who can find the answer.

An ancient journal, a Sioghra necklace and a special mark force life-altering decisions for a girl who grew up unprepared to fight for her life or others.

All secrets have a cost and Rouge's determination to find the truth can only lead to trouble...or something even more sinister.

RADIUM HALOS - THE SENSELESS SERIES
Book 1 is FREE:

Book Blurb:

Everyone needs to be a hero at one point in their life.

The small town of Elliot Lake will never be the same again.

Caught in a sudden thunderstorm, Zoe, a high school senior from Elliot Lake, and five of her friends take shelter in an abandoned uranium mine. Over the next few days, Zoe's hearing sharpens drastically, beyond what any normal human being can detect. She tells her friends, only to learn that four others have an increased sense as well. Only Kieran, the new boy from Scotland, isn't affected.

Fashioning themselves into superheroes, the group tries to stop the strange occurrences happening in their little town. Muggings, break-ins, disappearances, and murder begin to hit too close to home. It leads the team to think someone knows about their secret - someone who wants them all dead.

An incredulous group of heroes. A traitor in the midst. Some dreams are written in blood.

## Courage Runs Red
The Blood Red Series
Book 1 is FREE

What if courage was your only option?

When Kallie lands a college interview with the city's new hot-shot police officer, she has no idea everything in her life is about to change. The detective is young, handsome and seems to have an unnatural ability to stop the increasing local crime rate. Detective Liam's particular interest in Kallie sends her heart and head stumbling over each other.

When a raging blood feud between vampires spills into her home, Kallie gets caught in the middle. Torn between love and family loyalty she must find the courage to fight what she fears the most and possibly risk everything, even if it means dying for those she loves.

Daughter of Darkness
Victoria

*Only Death Could Stop Her Now*
The Daughters of Darkness is a series of female heroines who
may or may not know each other, but all have the same father,
Vlad Montour.
Victoria is a Hunter Vampire

# Free Books:

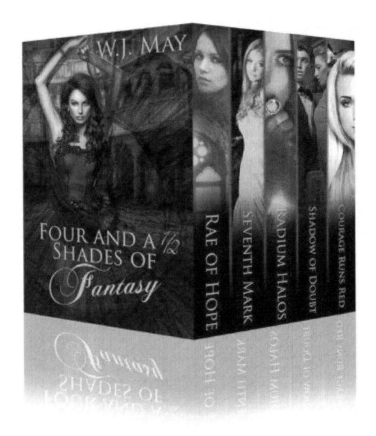

Four and a Half Shades of Fantasy

# TUDOR COMPARISON:

**Aumbry House**—A recess to hold sacred vessels, often found in castle chapels.
Aumbry House was considered very special to hold the female students - their sacred vessels (especially Rae Kerrigan).

**Joist House**—A timber stretched from wall-to-wall to support floorboards.
Joist House was considered a building of support where the male students could support and help each other.

**Oratory**—A private chapel in a house.
Private education room in the school where the students were able to practice their gifting and improve their skills. Also used as a banquet - dance hall when needed.

**Oriel**—A projecting window in a wall; originally a form of porch, often of wood. The original bay windows of the Tudor period. Guilder College majority of windows were oriel.
Rae often felt her life was being watching through one of these windows. Hence the constant reference to them.

**Refectory**—A communal dining hall. Same termed used in Tudor times.

**Scriptorium**—A Medieval writing room in which scrolls were also housed.
Used for English classes and still store some of the older books from the Tudor reign (regarding tatùs).

**Privy Council**—Secret council and "arm of the government" similar to the CIA, etc... In Tudor times, the Privy Council was King Henry's board of advisors and helped run the country.

# Don't miss out!

Click the button below and you can sign up to receive emails whenever W.J. May publishes a new book. There's no charge and no obligation.

**Sign Me Up!**

http://books2read.com/r/B-A-SSF-HUDJ

BOOKS 2 READ

Connecting independent readers to independent writers.

Did you love *Last One Standing*? Then you should read *Christmas Before the Magic* by W.J. May!

**Learn how it all began ... before the magic of tatùs.**

When Argyle invites his best friend, Simon Kerrigan, home for the Christmas holidays, he wants to save Simon from staying at Guilder Boarding School on his own.

Simon comes along and doesn't expect to find much more excitement in the tiny Scottish town where Argyle's family lives. Until he meets Beth, Argyle's older sister. She's beautiful, brash and clearly interested in him.

When her father warns him to stay away from her, Simon tries, but sometimes destiny has a hope of it's own.

*The Chronicles of Kerrigan Prequel is the beginning of the story before Rae Kerrigan. This Christmas Novella is the start (but it may not be the end...)*

| The | Chronicles | of | Kerrigan | Series |
|---|---|---|---|---|
| Rae | | of | | Hope |
| Dark | | | | Nebula |
| House | | of | | Cards |
| Royal | | | | Tea |
| Under | | | | Fire |
| End | | in | | Sight |
| Hidden | | | | Darkness |
| Twisted Together | | | | |

# Also by W.J. May

**Bit-Lit Series**
Lost Vampire
Cost of Blood
Price of Death

**Blood Red Series**
Courage Runs Red
The Night Watch
Marked by Courage
Forever Night

**Daughters of Darkness: Victoria's Journey**
Huntress
Coveted (A Vampire & Paranormal Romance)
Victoria

**Hidden Secrets Saga**
Seventh Mark - Part 1
Seventh Mark - Part 2
Marked By Destiny
Compelled
Fate's Intervention
Chosen Three

**The Chronicles of Kerrigan**
Rae of Hope
Dark Nebula
House of Cards
Royal Tea

Under Fire
End in Sight
Hidden Darkness
Twisted Together
Mark of Fate
Strength & Power
Last One Standing
Rae of Light

**The Chronicles of Kerrigan Prequel**
Christmas Before the Magic

**The Hidden Secrets Saga**
Seventh Mark (part 1 & 2)

**The Senseless Series**
Radium Halos
Radium Halos - Part 2
Nonsense

**The X Files**
Code X
Replica X

**Standalone**
Shadow of Doubt (Part 1 & 2)
Five Shades of Fantasy
Glow - A Young Adult Fantasy Sampler
Shadow of Doubt - Part 2
Four and a Half Shades of Fantasy
Full Moon
Dream Fighter
What Creeps in the Night
Forest of the Forbidden

HuNted
Arcane Forest: A Fantasy Anthology
Ancient Blood of the Vampire and Werewolf

54040019R00117

Made in the USA
Lexington, KY
04 August 2016